A Mistake of Murder

A Jan Christopher Mystery

Helen Hollick

A Mistake of Murder
A Jan Christopher Mystery - Episode 3
By Helen Hollick

978-1-7399371-6-4 A Mistake of Murder (paperback)
978-1-7399371-7-1 A Mistake of Murder (e-book)

Published by Taw River Press 2023
https://www.tawriverpress.co.uk

PREVIOUSLY

THE JAN CHRISTOPHER COSY MYSTERY SERIES SET IN THE 1970S

A MIRROR MURDER - Episode 1

Eighteen-year-old library assistant Jan Christopher's life is to change when her uncle, DCI Toby Christopher, gives her a lift home after work. Driving the car, is his new Detective Constable, Laurie Walker – and it is love at first sight for the young couple. But will a blossoming romance survive a police investigation into murder?

A MYSTERY OF MURDER - Episode 2

Will the discovery of a murder spoil Christmas for Jan Christopher and her boyfriend DS Laurie Walker – or will it bring them closer together? Join Jan (and an owl and a teddy bear) in Devon for a Christmas to remember.

TO FOLLOW:

Jan 4: A Meadow Murder

Jan 5: A Memory of Murder

READERS' COMMENTS for *A MIRROR MURDER* (episode 1)

"I sank into this gentle cosy mystery story with the same enthusiasm and relish as I approach a hot bubble bath, (in fact this would be a great book to relax in the bath with!) and really enjoyed getting to know the central character, a shy young librarian, and the young police officer who becomes her romantic interest. The nostalgic setting of the 1970s was balm, so clearly evoked, and although there is a murder at the heart of the story, it was an enjoyable comfort read." *Debbie Young, author of the Sophie Sayers cosy mysteries*

"A delightful read about a murder in North-East London. Told from the viewpoint of a young library assistant, the author draws on her own experience to weave an intriguing tale." *Richard Ashen – South Chingford Community Library*

"Well-paced with action interspersed with red herrings, shady suspects, and some nice passages of information which, ultimately are inconsequential, but are actually very interesting. Characterisations are excellent – especially Aunt Madge! I love Aunt Madge!"

"An enjoyable read with a twist in who done it. I spent the entire read trying to decide what was a clue and what wasn't... Kept me thinking. I call that a success."

"A delicious distraction... What a lovely way to spend an afternoon!"

To all library assistants everywhere
Thank you

1

NEW YEAR, 1972

On the first day of January 1972 (about 1.30 a.m.) I went, tired but happy, up to the guestroom at my boyfriend's parents' lovely old Devon farmhouse and, kicking off my high-heeled shoes (very smart, but very uncomfortable), flopped, exhausted onto the bed. We'd been to a wonderful village party, and I must admit I'd indulged in more Babycham than perhaps I should have done. I love Babycham, which was launched as a 'Champagne Perry' in the year I was born, 1953. (Although, naturally, I didn't drink it until a good few years later.) I especially like it when a morello cherry, stabbed onto the end of a wooden cocktail stick, is added. The cherry soaks up the taste of the 'champagne' – delicious!

After kissing and hugging everyone at midnight, we had all joined hands to sing *Auld Lang Syne*, and then we formed a long line and danced the conga up and down the village street. (Which was why my feet were hurting. Conga and high heels really do *not* mix.)

But if you can't enjoy yourself at New Year, when can you?

I reached across the pillow to give a hug to my

teddy, Bee Bear, resplendent in the new, yellow and black striped knitted jumper 'he' had been given as a Christmas present, and found a small velvet pouch tied around his neck with a silk ribbon. I opened it and found a heart-shaped box. Inside, a diamond ring and a slip of paper rolled up small. It read:

Will you marry me?
With all my love,
Laurie. XXX

I squealed and, shoeless, ran to his bedroom, threw my arms around his neck and yelled, at the top of my voice, "YES!"

Mr and Mrs Walker came hurrying from their room to see what the noise was about, and there followed more hugs and kisses, which then led to us all trooping downstairs again for some more bubbly. I think we got to bed by about three.

I did have a tiny niggling doubt about my hasty acceptance come the cold light of day. (I read that 'cold light' phrase in a book somewhere, no idea where, but it sounded good so I remembered it.) Laurie – Laurence Walker – was a newly promoted Detective Sergeant, a policeman in the North London suburb town of Chingford where I lived with my Uncle Toby and Aunt Madge. They were also my guardians. Uncle Toby – Tobias Christopher – was a Detective Chief Inspector, Laurie's 'Guvnor'. I'd lived with my uncle and aunt ever since I was five years old, having been orphaned when my father (also a policeman) had been murdered and my mother, well, all I know about her is that she died not long after Dad had been fatally shot. So I knew quite a bit about living with a policeman. And even though in January 1972 I was still quite young (about to turn nineteen) and still naïve, I had already encountered more than my fair share of unpleasant murders.

Did I want to be a policeman's wife? Were the tragedies of my past things I ought to consider for the future? What if Laurie was killed, callously murdered on his own front doorstep as my father had been? I didn't want to be a young widow dressed in black, dabbing my eyes with a lace handkerchief at a graveside in a bitter cold wind or pouring rain... Then I figured I was being over-dramatic and silly.

I loved Laurie, and he loved me. I would be safe with both him *and* Uncle Toby to look after me, wouldn't I?

But two days later, when I returned to work as a library assistant at our local South Chingford Library in north-east London, murder was waiting in the wings to shatter my confidence and pour a bucket-load of water on my happiness...

2

BACON AND LASAGNE

Getting up to go to work on a dreary, raining, grey-as-Welsh-slate January morning, was not easy. Especially as the day before, Laurie and I had driven all the way home to London from Devon. It had taken us seven hours because of the rubbish weather (it had poured the entire journey) and the amount of post-Christmas and New Year traffic on the road. The one thing that had me feeling eager to get out of bed, however, was the diamond ring on my left-hand ring finger. I was looking forward to sharing my engagement news with my co-workers at the library. It would have been jollier if the sun had been shining in a crisp, bright, winter-blue sky, though.

And if I hadn't missed the bus.

I waited ten minutes at the bus stop, gave up, decided to walk, and of course, just as I was too far to run on to the bus stop ahead, the next bus sailed past. I was, needless to say, somewhat soggy by the time I reached the library in Hall Lane. Even though my see-through plastic mac and sou-wester-type hat did all they were expected to do, my tights, shoes and feet were soaked. Just as well I kept comfortable, indoor 'work' shoes and spare tights in my staff room locker.

The girls I worked with were delighted with my news, and most admiring of my ring, which rather splendidly sparkled beneath the library's array of bright, overhead lighting.

"Have you a wedding date yet?" they all wanted to know. As it happened, we were all ladies together, the previous male librarian having left us last summer, (thank goodness, he was a miserable so-and-so) so talk of a forthcoming wedding was an exciting topic. I explained that we hadn't got even a tentative date as we wanted to wait and save a deposit for a house, which meant that I didn't expect to walk up the aisle on my uncle's arm for a couple of years, as Laurie had also suggested that we marry on the weekend nearest my twenty-first birthday, January 31st 1974.

That birthdate of mine is why my full name is 'January'. I was one of premature twins, my sister got the name 'June' for when we were conceived and I was lumbered with the month we were born. June died when we were quite young – but that's a gloomy topic, I'd rather talk about my engagement. The only problem: I didn't want to wait that long. 1974 was a long way off when it was only just, by a couple of days, 1972.

The library opened to the public at 10 a.m. so we had an hour to tidy the shelves. I'd been allocated the cookery section which was a bit boring as, unlike my aunt, I was a hopeless cook, but tucked away behind the bookshelves at the far end of the library I spent a good while browsing through a book of wedding cake designs. I wasn't so impressed when, in another book, *Breaking Out A Brilliant Breakfast*, I discovered someone had disgustingly used a rasher of uncooked bacon as a bookmark. Fortunately, it wasn't *too* mouldy, but the book was ruined.

Mondays and Thursdays were my late nights. The library is open from 10 a.m. to 8 p.m. on weekdays, except Wednesday when we are closed all day, and 10 to 5 on Saturdays. We work two of the late nights and have a half-day on the weeks when we're working an alternate Saturday. It all adds up to a seventy-two-hour fortnight – which under normal office-based employ would be the standard thirty-six hour week, just a bit jumbled up schedule-wise. This was going to be a long week, what with the two eight o'clocks and the coming Saturday. But my half-day on Friday was something to look forward to. Laurie was hoping to get the same afternoon off so that we could do something nice together. His work hours rarely added up to anything even approaching sensible. Policemen, like many other public services – nurses, ambulance drivers, firemen and such – rarely have the luxury of a standard week.

I was serving behind the U-shaped public counter for the morning, a bit of a bind as it was bound to be busy, but several nice regulars noticed my ring and wished me congratulations. One or two asked me if I'd had a good Christmas, and it was satisfying to truthfully answer 'Yes' for a change.

We all do it, smile and say what a wonderful Christmas, Easter or summer holiday we've had, even though in retrospect we'd not had as good a time as we'd originally hoped. But it seems so ungenerous to reply, 'No it was awful', doesn't it? A *stiff upper lip* Britishness, I suppose; we don't tend to whinge when someone asks the question they really don't want to hear the answer to. And if they *do* answer truthfully, how many of us figuratively roll our eyes and wish we hadn't asked in the first place?

I spent the afternoon in the office processing the

new books, which had come in just before the Christmas break. This could be interesting, depending on the books. One of the perks of working in a library, we get first pick of the new arrivals. The downside: my locker was stuffed with new books that I want to read.

The time between 5.30 and 7 p.m. was always the worst. It dragged, especially if the evening was quiet. There was always a rush just gone seven, though, and we dreaded it when people came in after 7.30 because no one could ever seem to choose books to read in twenty-five minutes.

I have a recurring nightmare: the hands on the clock on the wall are at 8 p.m. There are queues of people. I am on my own and I'm shouting, "We are closing! We are closing!" But more and more people are coming in... I slam the main doors shut and bolt them, but undeterred and determined to get their books, people start to climb in through the windows... Utterly absurd as the windows are high and narrow, but as a nightmare it's terribly unsettling.

Thankfully, this night it was fairly quiet, the longest queue we had was four people, and that was during the fifteen-minute tea break.

At about 7.15 one lady, who had grown up in Devon, wanted to chat so I grabbed a handful of books and toddled off to put them where they belonged on the shelves and she walked round with me – that way, we could natter but I was still working. I told her about our trip onto Exmoor and Dunkery Beacon where we'd braved a Christmas picnic despite the steady bluster of a bitter cold wind that had blown in straight off the sea. Probably all the way from North America as far as I knew.

"We were utterly mad," I laughed. "Huddled under blankets, shivering with cold, but laughing our socks off. Turkey sandwiches and mince pies on the highest point of North Devon."

She was quiet a moment, then said, "But Dunkery, that part of Exmoor, is in Somerset not Devon."

I looked at her aghast. "Is it really? My Aunt has a watercolour painting she did on her honeymoon and she's always said that it's of Dunkery on Exmoor in Devon." Then I giggled wickedly. "You wait until I tell her that she's got something wrong for once. I'll be able to tease her for months about this."

By almost eight o'clock there was the inevitable person who had left things to the last minute and was dithering about which book to take home, but he took the hint when Pamela, our Head Librarian, started to switch the lights off.

I only just caught the bus – I had to run the last few yards, but the conductor, bless him, delayed those few vital seconds so, puffing like a labouring steam locomotive climbing up over the great height of Shap Fell in the North of England, I made it onto the bus and slumped into a vacant seat. (I'd walked on Shap with my uncle and aunt – believe me it's high. In the days of steam it used to be notorious for the 1:75 gradient where trains heading north often needed assistance from another engine to reach the top.)

"Saw you coming, love," the conductor grinned, "so held it for you. Usual? The Ridgeway?"

I knew him fairly well, as he was often on this evening route of the 69 bus from somewhere-or-other in London to North Chingford. He was a friendly, good-looking man. I think his name was Joe – I'd heard someone call him that once. He often held the bus if he saw me coming. He was nice, friendly and chatty and I did sometimes wonder if he fancied me, which was extremely flattering but I never gave him any reason to be hopeful – too old for me for a start, he must have been in his thirties.

The bus smelled of chips. Someone two seats in front of me was eating them out of the paper wrapping. The aroma suddenly made me realise how hungry I was, and I wondered what Aunt Madge had cooked for dinner.

"Had a good Christmas and New Year?" he – Joe? – asked as he twirled the handle on his ticket machine, rolled out the printed paper ticket and handed it to me.

"Yes, lovely, thank you. You?"

"I was working for most of it. I volunteered for the extra shifts. Need the money. And my sister had Mum for Christmas. She's elderly, disabled." He shrugged, "My mum that is, not my sister."

"If you're local I could add your mother to our library book delivery service. I take books to the housebound."

"She's not much of a reader. Prefers the telly, them daft soaps: Coronation Street with Elsie Tanner and what's-his-name? Ken Barlow, but thanks for the offer. That's where you work, then is it? The library?"

I confirmed I did, and he wandered up to the man with the chips, told him, somewhat gruffly, that passengers were not allowed to eat on the bus – then cheekily helped himself to a few. More people got on and off; at my stop two young men got on and bounded up the stairs, while Joe offered his hand to help me step down from the platform, which was nice of him.

"You got far to walk?" he asked, peering out into the darkness of the wintry night.

"No, I live just along here," I said, pointing.

"Ah, the posh places for the toffee-nosed."

I wasn't sure if he was laughing or sneering at me. I wanted to reply that I was not 'toffee-nosed' but was too embarrassed to say anything. I wasn't very good at confrontation, nor for sticking up for myself when I ought to. Did he really think that I was a snob? A spoilt rich kid? Although, I suppose the houses along this part of the Ridgeway were 'posh'; most of them four-bedroomed, several were detached, early Edwardian in style. One was even Victorian, so quite large and rambling. All had big front gardens and even bigger back gardens, so they looked posh to an outsider. Uncle Toby, even having the rank of Detective Chief Inspector, certainly wasn't posh or rich. 'Well off' perhaps, because of Aunt Madge? Being honest, yes, she *was* 'upper class', which others sometimes thought of as rich. She spoke well, the true 'Queen's English'. Knew her manners, but *wasn't* a snob. That's what I thought of as 'posh'. Someone who unjustly lorded it over others, making them feel small and insignificant. Pretending to be something they weren't in order to show off. Aunt Madge was not a bit like that. She called a spade a spade if she had to. I'll concede, though, she did so in a BBC accent.

I pulled my collar up round my neck as the wind unkindly buffeted me and turned away from the bus stop. I heard the bell ring, and Joe call, "Hold tight there!" and the red bus trundled off into the dark night, its windows lit by the cheery interior lights.

A delicious smell greeted me as I walked in. Lasagne. Aunt Madge was a superb cook, unlike me; I'm hopeless at even boiling eggs or making toast, I always manage to burn it.

Uncle Toby and Laurie were working late. There had been a spate of burglaries since October, elderly people answering their front door to a conman who tricked his way in, pretending to be the gas man come to read the meter. He'd ask to use the loo, or for a drink of water – or even tea, cheeky blighter, and while the old lady was preoccupied, go down her handbag or search through a few drawers. Then, all smiles and niceness, the woman totally unaware that she'd been robbed, he'd leave apologising for the disturbance.

He only stole from elderly ladies and only took cash, never anything that he could not dispose of quickly and efficiently – and without being traced, so no jewellery or pension books. But these old folks tended to keep a lot of money indoors. One lady had over £200 stolen. Most of the victims reported that the man knocked soon after they had arrived home from being out somewhere, which indicated that he was either waiting or had followed them. Having just got home his targets were usually flustered by someone knocking so soon at the door – and their handbags would still be prominent, in the hall or on the kitchen table, and always with a coin purse in it. This burglar knew what to do, had his timing down to a fine art.

While eating, I nonchalantly told my aunt what I had learned that evening about Exmoor.

"Oh, I know that," she said. "Dunkery *is* the highest point on Exmoor, and Exmoor is mostly in Devon but some of it is in Somerset, Dunkery included, but I used artist's licence to commemorate the fact that our honeymoon hotel was in Devon and placed Dunkery in Devon as well."

"So all this time I've been geographically duped?" I jokingly complained.

"You could have checked the facts in a guide book. You must have several in the library."

I tucked into the lasagne. I loved her dearly, but you couldn't win with my Aunt Madge.

3

B.D.S

I always looked forward to every third Tuesday. A chance to get out of the library to do something different. The Book Delivery Service was one of the nicer perks. Three of us had our own round, taking books to the housebound. Mohammed and Mountains: *If you can't come to the library, the library will come to you.* The job involved selecting suitable books during the morning for our ladies and gentlemen, and delivering them during the afternoon via a van driven by Harry. Most of the recipients were elderly, but I had two younger disabled ladies – one was lovely, one was a slight mitherer, but I didn't mind as my B.D.S. route got me out and about, and Harry, who was an enormous laugh, always insisted on stopping for a cuppa – a cup of tea, which *always* included a slice of cake.

Selecting the books took most of the morning, and I eked the task out as I didn't want to end up with spare time in which I'd have to deal with boring overdue cards or filing. I set aside suitable new books when they arrived from Central Library, and kept an eye out for useful returns when they came in – the three of us doing B.D.S. had our own shelf under the counter especially for these set-asides.

I had eight people registered for my round, with, in theory, twenty minutes for each call. In practice, most took more than that, plus there was travel time, and the tea break that we were entitled to have. Nearly all my people were easy to select books for; thrillers and 'whodunits', along with romances were a doddle to find because of the huge choice. We had an entire bay of Mills and Boon romances in the library. One lady borrowed six *every* day when we were open. Whether she *read* all six we never discovered.

Could anyone *really* read *six* romances in a day?

Laurie surprised me at midday, turning up out of the blue with the offer of a quick lunch up at the Royal Albert pub. We were delayed by another round of congratulations on our engagement from my colleagues, but the pub was only a few minutes' walk away from the library. Both of us had shepherd's pie and a half-pint of lemonade shandy. Half-pint because Laurie had to be back on duty and I knew, with all the tea I'd be offered during the afternoon, that if I drank too much, I'd be visiting the loo at every stop.

We exchanged a discreet kiss goodbye outside the back door into the library, which turned out to not be as discreet as we thought when my driver came early with the London Borough of Waltham Forest van. Only it wasn't Harry. The driver was Kevin, twenty or so years younger than fifty-five-year-old Harry. Harry was fun, Kevin, well, Kevin wasn't. I'd been out on the round with him twice before, and if we were short of time he'd knock the prospect of tea and cake on the head. Which was a shame, even though my expanding waistline was the better for it.

"What's all this then?" Kevin said as he finished

reversing into the library's side alley and climbed down from the driver's seat.

"Hello," I said, waggling my ring finger under his nose. "Look what I've got!"

He pretended to peer myopically at my ring. "Bit of a sparkler, eh? Get it from a Christmas cracker, did you?" He teased. "Congratulations t'you both. I hope I get an invite to the weddin'? Hope this young lady turns out to be better than my trouble an' strife, mate. An' don't have any tin lids, they bleed you dry of bread 'n honey."

I mentally translated the Cockney rhyming slang: 'trouble and strife' – wife. 'Tin lids' – kids. 'Bread and honey' – money. Although Kevin was not an East End Cockney; he'd told me the first time we'd met that he came from the West Country. I think he put the rhyming slang on for effect.

We chatted about weddings, Kevin and I, as we drove off to my first port of call, discussing the best reception venues in the area. Kevin suggested one of the private clubs. "Walthamstow Avenue Football Club's a good place. Got a good bar there, and plenty of room for a knees up."

"I think my aunt will probably prefer the Kingfisher Hotel or the Royal Forest Hotel, or perhaps the Essex Country Club," I said doubtfully. All three were fashionable places. Very expensive.

My first stop was at Esther Hargreaves' house. I grabbed the books from their box in the back, expertly carrying all ten in the crook of my arm while I negotiated her front gate, which had the most savage bite to its spring. The garden gate equivalent of a Rottweiler, it could take your fingers off if you weren't careful.

Esther was a lovely lady. Most on my round were O.A.Ps – Old Age Pensioners – but Esther was in her early forties, I think. She was disabled from when she had an accident falling off her horse and was confined to a wheelchair. She had a rather grand motorised one and whizzed around the ground floor of her house that had been especially converted for her benefit. I suppose she was lucky because she could still make full use of her upper body, but it must have been hard for a previously active woman to be so confined.

Aunt Madge had two horses. I rode out with her on my days off and at weekends, and I always felt uneasy about her after visiting Esther. Was Aunt Madge back from her ride that morning? Was she OK? Silly of course, but when you love someone, you naturally worry. Beside which, Esther had her fall whilst riding fast in a ladies' point-to-point race, not quite the same thing as ambling leisurely around the bridleways of Epping Forest.

Esther preferred historical fiction or autobiographies, and she was always quick with making her selections, so I was soon back in the van and we were off to Miss Lettie Guffner. She was an elderly sweetheart who always had the kettle on to offer a cup of tea, which I always refused. Her tea was disgusting. I'd tried it once – she used sterilised milk, which was revolting. She liked to read anything and everything except murders.

"Give me nightmares, them do," she declared every time I called. Bless her.

When I got back to the van Kevin was muttering crossly and fiddling with the ashtray, trying to prise it open. Harry had deliberately stuck it up with strong glue to stop other drivers filling it with cigarette butts, because he loathed the stink of them. Kevin smoked like a chimney, although he wasn't supposed to while out driving with us. We all turned a blind eye to his quick fags *outside* the van while we were in people's houses delivering their books. What we didn't see we didn't grieve over, even if he did smell like a tobacco factory. He also had awful yellow, nicotine-stained fingers and nails, but as he always wore driving gloves, they were out of sight as well.

Next, Mrs Markham, an elderly widow who liked what she called 'old fashioned love stories', by which I had soon discovered, when she first joined the round, that she meant, "Nothing with 'that sort of stuff' in it". 'That stuff', being a euphemism for sex.

The problem: I never read romances, so hadn't a clue what was or wasn't in them. I was usually safe with Mills and Boon, as all their books had to adhere to a strict and set formula, which meant *no* sex. A bit like the Hollywood movies where romantic scenes stop at the bedroom door, beds are always twin, not double, or one foot has to stay on the floor. Aunt Madge knew several Americans who told her that twin beds were usually confined to movies, children's rooms and guest bedrooms. Many an American, as with us Brits, (and I assume other countries around the world?) likes to snuggle, husband and wife, (or partners, not everyone is married nowadays) in a double bed.

Look at me writing about *beds*! That would not be approved of in a Mills and Boon romance. I do hope no one censors this chapter because of my mention of taboo subjects!

When I got back to the van, Kevin had managed to force the ashtray open. He'd broken it; the little drawer was cracked from top to bottom. I pretended not to notice. Harry would be furious.

Next stop. The difficult ones.

Naturally, I would never have publicly called the next three gentlemen on my route 'difficult', especially not in their hearing, although I must have mentioned it to Harry at some point in the past because it was he who'd nicknamed them 'The Three Diffies'. Sort of like *The Three Musketeers*, but in reverse. *All for none and none for all.* The three men detested each other, even though one was a next-door neighbour and the other two were twin brothers who shared a house.

Grumpy bachelor 'Diffie', Mr Paul Norton's preference was for thrillers and science fiction. As I am a sci-fi 'nut' I found him quite easy to cater for book-wise, but he was not a pleasant man. Somewhat pompous and arrogant, he *always* found fault with the books I had previously brought him, pulling the writing and the plots apart as if he were a leading review critic. I mean, in my view, to say that writers like Robert Heinlein, Arthur C. Clarke and the great Anne McCaffrey were terrible writers was sacrilege!

On my last visit he had insisted that McCaffrey's *The Ship Who Sang* was, 'Disjointed and poorly written.' What? That title was one of her best. It's a story about the relationship between a cyborg ship (Brain Ship) and her captain. McCaffrey questions and explores what it means to be physically disabled but brilliant mentally. I wish I was clever enough to have thought up the idea.

I wanted to write. My first novel about a rogue hero space smuggler, Radger Knight, (Radger to rhyme with badger) was almost finished, and I would have loved to discuss it with someone – but Mr Norton would never be that 'someone' because of his unjustified scathing opinions. He always asked for *more* books by these same authors, so I soon realised that he was only showing off with a pretence of knowing what he was talking about. That 'empty vessels make the most noise' syndrome.

I mentioned him to Aunt Madge once, and she suggested that perhaps he was lonely, that his attitude was his way of attempting to initiate conversation and adult debate. She might have been right but when I tried, once, engaging with his criticism by challenging him, he told me I was an ignorant girl and to stick to 'silly romances or that Jackie comic rubbish.' Let me make this clear here and now. Jackie was a magazine *not* a comic.

We also went through the usual routine of Mr Norton thumping on the adjoining wall because next door's TV was so loud. I repeated, as I always did, that Mr Duffield was stone deaf, so wouldn't hear.

And Mr Norton replied, as he always did, "It's the *bang, bang, bang* of the guns from those ruddy westerns he watches that get me. So help me, one of these days I'll lose my temper with him about the noise."

Next door to him, the Twin Diffies. Although, to be fair, only one was difficult in the true sense. George and Gerald: identical twin brothers as far as looks were concerned, but for personality, as different as chalk is to Cheddar cheese. They shared a house but kept themselves isolated from each other. Gerald lived upstairs, George, downstairs, with scheduled times for using the bathroom, although there was a second, downstairs loo and upstairs the box bedroom had been fitted out as a kitchen. The front room downstairs was George's bedroom, the back room his living room. And the same upstairs for Gerald. Even the gardens were divided. Gerald did not like gardening, so he had the front garden, which consisted entirely of paving and low-growing shrubs. George preferred flowers, any sort, as long as they were pretty. He also grew vegetables and when they were in season often gave me things to take home: tomatoes, peas in their pods, little new potatoes, cucumbers from his greenhouse. I didn't need them, for Aunt Madge had her own allotment area at the end of the garden, but I took the veg and passed it to a grateful Harry, who lived in a block of flats and only had a balcony big enough for a few flowerpots.

They were both difficult to choose books for because of different reasons. George devoured westerns, which were thin on the ground to find as he had six books at a time. I'm sure he'd read quite a few of them more than once, but his memory was not good, so he never seemed to notice. Gerald would only read non-fiction. He tended to be fussy and (I probably shouldn't say this) he was an intellectual snob. The opposite of his brother. The only thing they had in common was their animosity towards each other – and Mr Norton next door.

I was always careful to ensure that I alternated which brother I visited first, otherwise Gerald complained. Today, George's turn first. He let me in at the front door with a cheery smile and offered to take the heavy box of books from me, bless him, but he hobbled around with the aid of a walking stick, so I always said that I could manage. Working in a library is not the easy job people think it is. Books are heavy. We carried armfuls at a time, heaved boxes about, pushed trolleys, were on our feet for much of the day, and walked miles round all those shelves.

The TV, as heard from next door, was blasting away in George's living room – literally blasting, the volume loud because of George's deafness. Today, a western series was just finishing, *Bonanza,* instantly recognisable by its zingy theme tune. For my visit, George did turn the telly off, which was a relief as I would never have been able to shout over its high volume.

I could hear a cat meowing. While George looked at his books, I gazed around the room. Monty, George's ginger cat, was usually curled asleep on one of the two armchairs. No sign of him today.

"Where's Monty?" I shouted, pointing to his chair.

"Eh?" George said. "I haven't seen him since breakfast."

The meowing grew more frantic, with a scratching sound joining in. George followed me as I went to the cupboard under the stairs and opened it. Out sprang Monty, tail lashing furiously as he rushed to the kitchen and I heard the cat flap go *click-bang*.

"I expect he is about to burst his boiler, desperate for a wee." George laughed. "Poor puss. I didn't hear him."

I didn't say anything, but I did wonder how long the poor cat would have stayed locked in if today hadn't been Book Delivery day.

Going back to choose his books, George asked me if I had enjoyed Christmas, and congratulated me on my engagement, then told me, yet again, how it amused him that he loved great westerns and had worked for Great Western.

"The railway," he chuckled. "I was a train driver. Took many a train down to Truro from Paddington. All through the War an' all. I got a medal when we were attacked by a German. Did I ever tell you?" (He had, several times.) "It were between Taunton and Tiverton. Damn thing came after us, guns blazing *ack, ack, ack*. Well, I opened my loco up, and went hell for leather, my fireman shovelling coal into the firebox like there'd be no tomorrow. We had a strict speed limit, mind you, but on this occasion I ignored it. Opened her up an' got her up to more than ninety miles an hour. Ninety! Fair rocketed along, we did, with that Jerry *ack, ack, ack* shooting at us, windows shattering, bullets pinging off the cream and brown woodwork. I had to start slowing before the tunnel, but judged it just right and brought her to a halt *in* the tunnel. Outsmarted that German so-an'-so. Coaches were shot up good an' proper, a couple of passengers injured, nothing serious. I saved us from the worst. Only one person copped it. A lady in the rear carriage. I had to do an emergency stop, of course. Slam the brakes on. Passengers got bumped and bruised, but she fell, hit her head. Split her skull right open. Died instant. Pretty little thing, too, she were. Left a couple of kiddies behind, so they said." Abruptly, he changed the subject. I could tell that he was upset by the lady's death, so understood his consternation. "I'll take these ones, dear, they look good."

The cat flap clicked again and Monty returned, in a better humour. He twined around my legs while I tickled his chin, then jumped up onto the table and promptly sat himself down in the book box in the space where I hadn't yet put the returned books. He sat there, giving his whiskers a good polishing. I hadn't the heart to move him until he'd completed his ablutions. Why do cats so enjoy squeezing into awkward places to wash?

George put the books he wanted on his bookshelf and turned the TV on again. A resounding thumping sounded, almost immediately, from the wall adjoining next door – Mr Norton again – and simultaneously from the room above.

Out of sheer reciprocal b-mindedness, George rapped on the wall with the handle of his stick. "He's a miserable geezer next door. I reckon some sort of bad fairy cursed him when he were in his cradle. Either that or his mother dropped him on his head once too often. And as for him upstairs," he pointed upwards with his stick, "I 'spect his lordship'll be wanting you to go up. Better see to the old basket before he has a heart attack. Hah! I should be so lucky!"

"One of these days," I said to Monty as I lifted him out of the box and put him on his armchair so I could fill the gap with the books George was returning, "I'll not notice you and I'll carry you out to the van."

George chuckled. "I'll be reporting you to that young policeman of yours if you did. *Cat*nap not *kid*nap!"

4

AD NAUSEAM

Gerald was waiting for me, arms folded, at the top of the stairs. He didn't offer to take the box of books, but tutted and pointed to the table in his living room, indicating where I was to put it. "On the tablecloth, girl, not the wood."

I smiled. "Oh, yes of course, you don't want this lovely wood scratched do you. Is it mahogany?" I had no idea what sort of wood it was, it could have been plastic for all I knew, but I'd learnt, a while ago, how to backfoot him.

"It's walnut," he answered, unconvincingly. He had no more idea than I had.

Gerald had four books so I took eight to give him a choice. Non-fiction only. *'Serious stuff, not that fiction nonsense.'*

He would sit down at the table (never offered me a seat) and solemnly take each book out of the box to studiously read the blurb on the back cover. Then do the same with the flap inside the front cover. Usually tutting about something he disagreed with. Then he would read a couple of paragraphs from the first chapter. If satisfied, he rose from his chair and placed the books he wanted on the coffee table beside his armchair. If not, they went back into the box.

"There are cat's hairs in this box," he complained, giving a little huff of disapproval.

"Yes, Monty decided to sit in it. Such a dear little cat, don't you think?"

"No. It's an annoying *Felis catus*, the only domesticated species in the family *Felidae*. The thing is more trouble than it is worth. Cats ought to be classed as vermin. Dogs too."

I almost said, *What about grumpy old men*? Managed to bite it back.

I could see down into the back garden from where I stood. George was pottering up the path towards his small greenhouse at the end, Monty beside him. Silly man had no coat on, and although the rain had stopped for a while it was still cold and damp outside. I kept a discreet eye as he could easily fall on the wet, slippery paving slabs. Gerald caught me looking.

"Nothing to see in that garden," he grumbled. "I keep my front garden tidy. *His* back garden is a jungle. Full of weeds, slugs and snails."

"Probably the occasional tiger as well?" I joked.

"Tigers? Don't talk nonsense, young lady. The *Panthera tigris* are found in India, not London suburbs. It is the largest of the genus *Panthera*."

I ignored the Latin and changed the subject. "I think your brother has some beautiful roses. They looked lovely back in the summer. Roses are the family *Rosaceae*, I believe? With something like over three hundred species." I only knew that because Aunt Madge loved her roses and knew all the names of the ones in our garden – and the garden next door.

Gerald snorted. "Typical! He goes outside and leaves that damn television of his blaring away. I have to struggle down every night to turn the wretched thing off. He's so senile he goes to bed and leaves the thing on. Does it deliberately to annoy me. He knows I have a heart condition. I refuse to have a television. Load of nonsense on it. I am *semper fidelis* to the Third Programme or the Home Service."

There was no point in my reminding him that these had changed to Radio 3 and Radio 4 back in 1967. Nor that I hadn't a clue, beyond roses, about Latin. He was always inserting little quotes wherever he could, *ad nauseam*. Ah! I know *that* one!

Poor George. He was deaf *and* forgetful and it was more likely that he couldn't hear the TV once he'd gone to bed.

"Told you that stupid joke about 'Great Western' and 'great westerns' again, did he? And that fiasco about the tunnel and the war? Oh, yes, I bet he did. Reiterates both over and over. All exaggerated. Probably even made it up. I'll take these four. The one about Roman Britain might be interesting, although there is not much I do not know about the Romans. *Experto credite*. I should have been an Oxford master, you know, lecturing in the Classics, but the war got in the way. Ended up teaching snot-nosed grubby monsters who did not know Octavian from Augustus at the Grammar School. I'm not sure about this English Civil War one. What a shambles *that* was. Useless king. Charles should have been beheaded right from the start, in my opinion."

I nearly said, *weren't Octavian and Augustus the same person?* but guessed I'd then receive a long-winded lecture on the first Emperor of Rome and the shenanigans that went on prior to that event. Caesar, Mark Anthony, Cleopatra – Elizabeth Taylor, Richard Burton and all that lot.

I must have looked harassed as I put the heavy box of books back into the van parked a few doors away, because Kevin asked if I was all right. He didn't offer to come and help, though. I sighed, but then laughed as I shoved the used box to the back, and pulled the next one I would need to the front.

"The same conversations again," I said over my shoulder as he finally came to join me at the back of the van. "But I did get a slightly different version of the tunnel story today."

"Tunnel story?"

"Yes, during the war. George was a train driver. He stopped a train in a tunnel when a German plane was shooting at it."

"Oh? Where was this then?" Kevin shut the van's back door.

"Devon. Between Taunton and Tiverton. 1943 I think it was."

"Did anyone get hurt?"

"One woman died when she fell and cut her head open. It could have been much worse – that plane could have blown the whole train up. Shall we go for a cup of tea?" I said, changing the subject. "The Old Church Hall teas are really good, and the profits are for charity. Harry usually leaves the van here and we walk round the corner." Seeing his dubious look, I added, "They do home-made cakes too. I'll pay."

That perked him up. I guessed it would, but I don't know why I offered to foot the bill. I suppose I thought that out of politeness he'd at least insist on paying his share. I forgot that, unlike dear Harry, Kevin was not a nice, polite man.

The hall, built to the side of the Old Church, which sat atop the hill known as Chingford Mount, was a wooden building, with afternoon teas offered on Tuesdays and Thursdays by volunteer ladies of the Friends of the Old Church. It really is an *old* church, part of it dates back to the twelfth century. By 1904 it had been abandoned for the new church in North Chingford, and fell into dereliction, but was then rebuilt. I am not particularly a churchgoer, but I was fond of this lovely old place.

I ordered two teas and two slices of coffee and walnut cake from the lady behind the trestle table counter, and joined Kevin who had seated himself at a table. He was frowning, deep in thought, then suddenly jumped up again.

"I don't think I locked the van," he said. "I'd better check. Won't be a jiffy."

He was gone longer than I expected and came back red-faced, puffing from running and smacking his cap against his thigh, showering raindrops on the wooden church hall floor. "It's starting to rain again," he said as he grumpily slurped a gulp of his 'rosy lea' – which must have been cold by then – and bit into the cake. He grimaced. "Don't like coffee cake much." He ate it all, though.

"Harry usually keeps an umbrella in the back," I said, thinking that he could have fetched it. "Shall I get you a fresh tea, you've been gone quite a while."

"Yes. This one's like cold pond water. Didn't see no brolly. I had to nip into the bushes beside the Baptist church for a Jimmy Riddle, then some old biddy came out the church and fiddled with keys to lock the door. I had to squat down so she didn't see me. That's what took me so long."

I didn't know whether to believe him or not. More likely, he'd stopped to smoke a cigarette.

I know I said I'd pay, but he didn't offer to pay me back for the two cups of tea, or the cake; he merely drank his fresh tea, said we had to get a move on, and hurried off to open the van up. I nipped to the ladies out the back, hoping that by the time I'd finished the rain would have stopped. He could have just as easily made use of the gents, not the church bushes.

It hadn't stopped raining, but it had eased to a light drizzle. I pulled my coat up to my ears, ducked my head and ran.

Kevin didn't open the van door for me. I don't swear, well, not much, but Aunt Madge occasionally muttered under her breath a word which is entirely innocuous, but said quickly can sound similar to something naughty. I murmured it as I climbed into the cab and Kevin started the engine, not waiting for me to get settled.

I was beginning to not enjoy the afternoon as much as I usually did.

5

THE LITTLE LIBRARY

Friday Hill, a sort of suburb of Chingford, was a vast council estate, named for John Friday who held land there in the fifteenth-century; prior to that, it was known as Jackatt Hill. I only knew all this because my Uncle Toby, as well as being a brilliant Detective Chief Inspector, was a mine of useless miscellaneous information. The council estate was built after the war in 1945 when housing was desperately needed for all those poor families bombed out by the Blitz. Many a townie coming to Friday Hill thought they were in the middle of the countryside as they found themselves on the border of Essex and Epping Forest where there were cows roaming freely.

There is a local legend for the pub on top of the hill, The Sirloin. According to the tale, King Charles II stayed at the inn one night and enjoyed a meal of roast beef so much that he knighted it: "I dub thee Sir Loin!"

It's probably not true, but it is a good tale.

Mrs Westwood, my next call, lived in a romantic-sounding road, Withy Mead, that conjured up an image of willow trees – withies – swaying in a gentle breeze beside the water meadows where black and white cows would graze lazily beneath the summer sun, swishing their tails against bothersome flies. Swans would paddle in the river, gracefully dipping their heads as a clutch of cygnets scurried behind. In the distance, the soaring spire of a cathedral, its bells ringing out joyfully, the peal announcing the elation of a wedding... A fanciful image, and reminiscent of the sweeping water meadows near Salisbury Cathedral; nice to imagine but very far from reality. There wasn't a tree in sight anywhere along Withy Mead, let alone a graceful weeping willow. Friday Hill itself was, as the name suggested, a hill. A long, steep, hill with a small library at the top, but impossible for Mrs Westwood to get to because of her restricted mobility. She liked authors such as Georgette Heyer, Jean Plaidy, Daphne du Maurier and Catherine Cookson, so was easy to please.

I was a tad annoyed as I went to the back of the van to collect her bundle of books. There, admittedly hidden by an old blanket, was a gentleman's umbrella. Still, the rain had stopped so I didn't need it now.

From Mrs Westwood's house we went to the Little Library where Mrs Colchester was in charge, a lovely lady who would do anything for anyone. Friday Hill Library might be small but it was usually busy (a fact probably helped along by the chocolate biscuits that Mrs C would keep on the counter for anyone to help themselves to – although she did remove them once school was out and the children came in, as they tended to scoff the lot. 'Adults only' was her rule as far as biscuits were concerned).

The library itself was one room about the size of a fair-sized living room, with a stock cupboard, tiny kitchen and 'facilities' out the back. The books themselves did not have a wide range of choice, which is why South Chingford Library, (the parent library) made a Tuesday delivery every week to augment the limited stock. Once a year there was a modest change of stock. New for old, as it were.

Mrs C was a 'cosy grandma' sort of lady, with a round, jolly face and she was delighted to hear of my engagement; gave me a huge bear hug while admiring my ring.

"Tell your uncle," she said, after serving a customer who came in to collect a book reserved for him and left again, "that when I went to the cemetery to tend my hubby's grave last Sunday, I noticed a man loitering near the gates. I'm sure I saw the same man there on Boxing Day, too. He looked quite shifty."

"But there are probably quite a few people hanging around near cemeteries on those sort of days aren't there? People not sure whether to go in or not? People grieving, people wanting to be alone?"

"I thought the same when I saw him that first time, so thought nothing of it, but now I'm not so sure. He followed me for a little way, but turned back when he realised I had a car. I sat and watched him, pretending to sort my hair out in the mirror. He went back to the gates then followed another woman as she left the cemetery."

I offered a reasonable explanation. "Perhaps he was just bored and walking about. Could the woman have been his wife, perhaps?"

"I don't think so, he had been loitering around for a good fifteen minutes. If they knew each other why did he follow me? Why follow *behind* this other woman, not next to her? I just thought, in light of this spate of burglaries, that your uncle ought to know. He was about 5'9. My hubby's height. Slimmish build. I didn't see his face clearly. He had a hat, a cap, pulled well down. Dark blue trousers – I don't think they were black, and a dark overcoat. I did wonder if he was another of those pesky flashers who were using the

Forest last summer, but with these thefts going on... Is that your driver tooting out there? Certainly miss our Harry when he's not here, don't we?"

Kevin had carried the new book box in, taken the old books out and got straight back into the van. Because I had stayed to chat to Mrs C, he was now impatiently beeping the horn.

"I'd best go," I said. "I've still got one lady to visit. I'll tell Laurie or Uncle Toby about the man at the cemetery, don't worry."

It was probably uncharitable of me, but I couldn't help noticing that Kevin wore dark blue trousers. And he wore a cap.

6

'HOME JAMES'

My last lady was easy to cater for as she was an absolute sweetheart. Miss Catesby lived near the Old Church. Normally, it would have made sense to visit her straight after 'The Diffies' and before our tea break, but I'd changed the route six months ago because she had been offered the chance to be taken to a regular luncheon club every Tuesday by a friend who had a car. When she'd said, "I'll have to stop you calling, my dear," and explained why, with tears glistening in her eyes because she loved her books, I'd immediately suggested the change.

"No problem, Miss Catesby, I can make you the last of my calls, you're on the way back to the library, so it'll not be out of our way." She'd burst into tears and given me such a hug of gratitude. Bless her.

Today though, she was in a tizzy as she answered the front door to my ringing the doorbell.

"Oh, Jan dear! Come in, come in – I feel awful!" She was fluttering about like a moth caught in a jam jar.

"Whatever is the matter Miss Catesby? Are you ill?"

"No, no, nothing like that, but my luncheon friend forgot to buy your chocolate for me. I'm so sorry. I haven't any for you this time. I'll quite understand if you don't want to leave me any books today."

She regularly bought two bars of Cadbury's Old Jamaica chocolate, one for herself, one for me to share with Harry. She claimed, "My special treat to look forward to. Makes me feel like a lady pirate sailing off with Errol Flynn."

In return I always told her off, because I knew she couldn't afford two bars of chocolate at 9p each on her meagre pension, but she insisted. I do feel mean, though, as Harry didn't like the raisins in it, but I loved them, so I would scoff the lot. (On top of the fattening home-made cake at the church hall? I know, I'm shocking aren't I?)

Today, I laughed and patted her arm. "Please don't worry. The amount of weight I put on at Christmas, I shouldn't be eating chocolate."

"Yes but, dear, it's my way of saying thank you. Look..." she reached for her handbag on the hall telephone table. "If I give you the money, could you buy something for yourself?"

"Absolutely not. You put that money away."

"But..."

"No buts. If it makes you feel better, why not get me two bars next time?"

She beamed a bright smile, her blue eyes twinkling. "What a good idea. I'll do that then." She put her bag back on the telephone table next to one of those Victorian round, glass-domed taxidermy ornaments. This one was a stuffed puffin and had belonged to her father. She'd rescued it from house clearance soon after he'd died. Personally, I'd have buried it along with him.

If I hadn't been too delayed by my previous calls I often stayed to talk to Miss Catesby, and of course, today she wanted to hear all about my Christmas and

New Year in Devon – and had to inspect my engagement ring. She was so excited and delighted for me. She ushered me into the lounge, a lovely through room that had light all day from the front and the back. At one end she'd lit the fire, which was blazing merrily. 'So much cosier than the gas fire,' she always said – there was a gas fire in the front 'dining room' half of the room, both of which, I gathered, she rarely used.

Her own beau was Albert Barrowstone – she'd been engaged to him, but he'd been killed at the Somme. As happened back then, ladies left without their fiancés were not expected to find anyone else – there were very few 'else' left alive after that dreadful war. She had a photograph of him on the mantlepiece, which had been lightly 'touched up' to give it a cheery feel of colour. He looked most handsome. A second black and white photo on the sideboard was of them both, with her mother looking extremely prim and proper, as older ladies did back then. Next to Albert was his brother. The two men looked very much alike.

"The photographs were taken on the day we got engaged," she had told me. "He was quite a few years older than I was, but that did not matter. The next day, the two of them went off to join their regiments. I have a photograph of my Albert upstairs, looking smart in his uniform. I was so proud of him. Still am." She'd paused a while when telling me this, and I'd seen a tear glistening in the corner of her eye. Then she'd added, "His brother came back to his young lady. Albert didn't come back to me."

She often talked to the photographs, and I assume to the one she had upstairs beside her bed. Poor lady, she must have been so sad and lonely, all these years, without him.

Noticing the photo on the mantlepiece, I wondered how I would feel if I lost Laurie were he involved in an accident or something, but I immediately thrust the thought away. Too awful to think about. I loved him. Was certain that I loved him and that I had made the right decision. No doubts. Certain.

Miss Catesby purred over my ring, delighted for me. "My Albert would be so pleased for you my dear – wouldn't he Poppy puss?" From one of the armchairs arranged before the blazing fire, a green-eyed black and white cat stared at me with solemn regard as Miss Catesby stroked her head, eliciting a loud, humming purr of contentment.

"Poppy is my cherished companion," Miss Catesby added, giving the cat another stroke. "She shares the fire with me, and this is her chair." Miss Catesby was quiet a moment, then added, "It would have been Albert's chair, were he here, but... Oh well, now, what books have you brought for me, my dear?"

With her back crooked from old age and hands gnarled from arthritis, Miss Catesby must have constantly been in a lot of discomfort, but she remained cheerful and never complained. I shouldn't, have done, but I usually washed and dried up any plates and cups that were in her kitchen sink while she selected her books. Harry knew I did this and sometimes came in to help. (He once even trundled her wheezy old vacuum cleaner around the lounge for her.) I always replenished the coal scuttle for her as well, filling it from the coal bunker in the garden beside the back door.

Kevin would never have helped out with any chores, and would have moaned like mad about time wasting if he knew of my helping out, so I'd said nothing to him about the friendly 'extras'. I wonder what his wife thought of him? I doubted that he ever helped with housework, shopping or their three children. I could imagine him being selfish and lazy at home. The sort of man who came home and expected his dinner to be ready and waiting, who never helped with washing up or doing the shopping. Selfish.

Miss Catesby read absolutely anything. I did wonder, sometimes, that perhaps she didn't read the four books I left her, merely wanting them in order to have someone call in for company? I'd never have dreamed of challenging her about it though – it wasn't important and it made no difference to me whether she read them or not.

I couldn't blame her for wanting the company, for aside from the daily Meals on Wheels and her weekly luncheon club with her friend, she saw almost no one else the rest of the week. Her immediate neighbours were a youngish couple out at work all day, and in winter were never in their garden. Her house was in the corner of a cul-de-sac, so no passing traffic, although there was an alleyway which ran alongside her house and garden and then beside the church to the main road, but apart from Sundays it was not a busy route as it didn't form much of a shortcut to anywhere. Originally, the cul-de-sac would have been the garden of the vicarage at the other end of the close, and the vicarage was now converted into flats, so I guess the alley used to be the vicar's personal route to the church.

However, I couldn't stay forever and it was already dark outside, so I had to bid the dear old lady farewell, and remind her to lock the front door and put the chain on. She waved to me from the front bay window, Poppy cuddled in her arms.

"Took your time," Kevin grumbled as, after I'd dumped the returned books in their box in the back of the van, I shut the doors and clambered into the front passenger seat.

"Miss Catesby's lonely," I said by way of explanation.

"Not our job to be Social Services, 'specially not to old biddy westminsters."

I guessed he meant 'spinsters'.

He continued grumbling as he backed, badly, out of the cul-de-sac. "We're going to be late back if I don't put my foot down. It's almost five now. I'm supposed to finish at five-thirty, and after dropping you off, I have to drive back to the depot. Traffic will be dreadful. An' I'm off on leave. Got a train t'catch to Southampton, stay in a B and B overnight, then the ferry first thing. I'm due a long break starting the moment I knock off. Every year I go to the Isle of Wight with my mates. Sea fishing by day, round the pubs by night. Six of us. Best mates, best time of the year."

"What about your family?" I asked, looking at him askance. "Your wife and daughters?"

He scowled at me. "What about 'em? They are not interested in fishing. Been stuck with them all over Christmas. That were bad enough, I did m'duty, now it's *my* turn for some enjoyment. Lord knows I don't get much of it." He crunched the gears into place.

On the other hand, I thought, *his wife is probably as keen to be rid of him*. "Well, the library's only round the corner," I pointed out. "We'll be there in a few minutes." Assuming he didn't murder the clutch in the meantime.

He merely grunted and bumped the van up the kerb as he failed to manoeuvre carefully enough. Harry always reversed *in* so that the back of the van faced the house, making less distance for me to carry the books. Kevin, naturally, was not so thoughtful.

Trying to be jolly, I added, "And the porter will be there to help you unload, so Home James, and don't spare the horses!"

That was a favourite quote of Aunt Madge's, and she often sang it. I'd looked it up in one of the library's encyclopaedias. There were a couple of theories about the origin, but the consensus seemed to be that it was a music hall song from the 1890s about a woman's romantic date that had gone disastrously wrong. It was recorded in 1933 as a 78-RPM long-playing record, to be sold exclusively in Marks and Spencer's Department Stores. I'd told Laurie about it while we were down in Devon – after Aunt Madge and Uncle Toby had left for home before us just after Christmas because I'd shouted the quote out to them as they drove off. Laurie had laughed, gone straight to the piano in the farmhouse sitting room and promptly made up a suitable accompaniment to the words.

I smiled at Kevin, and in an attempt to lighten his bad mood, burst into song using Laurie's jaunty tune:

"Home, James and don't spare the horses,
This night has been ruined for me.
Home, James and don't spare the horses,
Oh, I'm ruined as ruined can be."

Laurie's voice was *much* more musical than mine, and Harry would have cheerfully joined in. Kevin merely grunted.

Back at the library, I left him to unload the boxes – that was his job, not mine – but as it was raining again I quickly nipped round the back of the van and retrieved the umbrella, which I ostentatiously brandished aloft.

"I'll borrow this if I may? I have to walk to the bus stop and don't want to get wet. I'll give it back to Harry next time I see him. Enjoy your fishing trip."

Kevin made no answer. Not even a surly grunt or

an excuse for apparently not seeing it, but then, the umbrella wasn't his, it belonged to Harry. It was a quality London store brand that had been given to Harry by his two daughters as a special 50th birthday present. It had his initials engraved on the silver ring beneath the handle: *H.L.J.*

He had privately confided to me that he couldn't be bothered with umbrellas, but it was useful to keep it in the van. "Don't let on to my kids, though," he'd said. "I'm not supposed to keep personal stuff in the van, but as it's usually only me who drives it... well, I can't be bothered to keep putting useful things in and out. I just have to trust no one nicks it." He'd laughed, "Mind, I wouldn't miss it."

A little uncharitably, I wondered if Kevin realised that the brolly was possibly worth a few bob because of the prestigious maker's label and the silver band.

7

RINGS AND THINGS

I shook the wet umbrella and folded it down as the 69 bus trundled along. The red Routemaster bus was fairly full, but a seat had become vacant right beside the conductor's platform, so I sat down and propped the wet brolly in the empty luggage space beneath the curve of the stairs. The bell rang twice, *ding-ding*, from upstairs and off we rumbled. I heard the conductor grumbling at someone upstairs – Joe, I recognised his voice. A moment later he came half-sliding, half-jumping down the stairs.

"Fares please! Any more fares? Have y'money ready. I ain't got time t'mess about." He saw me and his apparent irritation disappeared. He smiled. "Evenin' love. Nice t'see you. Usual?"

"Hello again," I said, as I paid for my ticket with the 5p coin I'd put specifically for this purpose in my coat pocket. "I don't usually see you on a Tuesday."

He gave me my bus ticket. "Na, I'm on an early shift today. This is my last run. I knock off at Chingford terminus as soon as I can sign off." He went on up the aisle. "Any more fares please? Any fares! Have y'money ready."

I shoved the ticket in my coat pocket, then relaxed into my seat. The end of a busy day. A hot bath and dinner cooked by Aunt Madge awaited me at home, plus the TV wasn't too bad on a Tuesday evening. Then suddenly I felt sick. Not the sort of sick where you're about to throw up, but the sort where your stomach churns and somersaults, your throat runs dry and blind panic sets in.

Sitting there, with my left hand resting on top of my handbag I stared down and saw it. Or rather, *didn't* see it.

My engagement ring was not on my finger.

I must have gasped aloud because the bus conductor peered round at me from where he was standing, two seats away. "You all right? You've gone as white as a sheet." He came and stood beside me.

"I've lost my engagement ring!" I blurted out, tears choking my voice. "My diamond ring!" I wiggled my naked fingers at him.

"Oh? Got engaged, did you? Missed out, 'ave I? You've gone an' broken m'heart!" He turned in time to see a schoolboy about to jump off before the bus had come to a halt at the next stop. Crossly, he shouted, "Oi! Boy! Hold tight there, bus 'asn't stopped yet, an' I'll be the one in trouble if you injure y'self."

The boy shouted something back, which I didn't hear.

"Cheeky beggar," Joe grumbled, "His mother ought to clip his ear more often." No one else got off or on, so he rang the bell and we were on our way again, lumbering slowly up the rising incline of the steep hill that was Chingford Mount.

"Now," Joe said, "take a couple of deep breaths. Think back. Where did you last have this ring of yours?"

The deep breaths helped, but not a lot.

"I had it earlier this afternoon when I was delivering library books to the housebound." Yes, I'd *definitely* had it when I was with George Duffield, as I remembered seeing the diamond flash when I was stroking Monty.

"And I had it on when I was with Mrs Colchester at Friday Hill because she said how pretty it was," I said, then laughed with relief. "Oh, I know where it is! I took it off when I did the washing up for old Miss Catesby. It's on her kitchen windowsill!"

"There you go, then. Not lost at all. Where does this Miss Catesby live?"

"She's right behind the Old Church in Vicarage Close, I'll get off there and pop round to see her."

"All sorted then, love." He grinned at me as the bus struggled up to the brow of the hill, although it managed, this time, to keep going. Quite often a bus would grind to a halt if too many passengers left their seats eager to alight quickly at the next stop. With the extra weight gathered on the rear platform, the buses couldn't always make it over the top of the hill, so amid much grumbling, everyone would have to get off and walk the rest of the way.

It hadn't occurred to me as I got off the bus – at the bus stop – and walked through the tree-lined alley beside the church, that dear Miss Catesby might not answer my knock at her front door.

Of course she wouldn't; it was January, and although only five-thirty it was already dark. What elderly person answers an unexpected caller when it's dark? I knocked several times, then bent down to call through the letterbox.

"Miss Catesby? It's me, Jan from the library. Are

you there?" Which was a silly thing to say, as of course she was there. Peering through the letterbox I could see a light on in her kitchen and back room, and I could hear that the TV was on.

I called again. Still no answer.

I started to feel worried – for the possibility of not being able to get my ring back and because a tragic memory suddenly resurfaced. Not that long ago Laurie and I had found an old lady dead –murdered – in her house. The lights had been on in *that* house… Although the front door had been wide open.

I knocked again. Louder. "Miss Catesby? Miss Catesby are you all right? It's only me, Jan from the library."

Beside the house was a short driveway leading to two garages. One was Miss Catesby's; the other belonged to the next door neighbour. Naturally, Miss Catesby had no car so her garage was only used for storage. I wondered if there might be a gate along the fence bordering her back garden. There was, but it was taller than me and firmly bolted. I rattled the latch a few times then called out again. "Miss Catesby? It's me, Jan Christopher. I left my ring on your windowsill this afternoon."

Oh, please, please answer! I thought, choking back fresh tears.

Then I heard a lady's voice behind me. I spun round, startled.

"Hello, can I help? I'm Miss Catesby's neighbour. Is there anything wrong?"

I explained the situation and the lady smiled pleasantly. "I've got a spare key. Hang on, I'll fetch it."

She disappeared into her house, came back and walked with me to Miss Catesby's front door. She opened it and reaching inside, flicked the hall light on. I would need to tell Miss Catesby off – she hadn't put the security chain on, although perhaps in this instance it was just as well, because if she *had* done so we'd not have been able to go in.

"Mary?" the neighbour called as we walked into the hall. "It's only me."

To my relief Miss Catesby came out of her kitchen. "Dorothy, I've been that worried, someone was knocking at my door and..."

I stepped forward. "Yes, it was me. I left my ring here."

"Oh, Jan dear. I didn't recognise your voice." Miss Catesby laughed and beckoned me inside. The neighbour left us to it, shutting the front door behind her.

"Where did you leave the ring? I'm *so* sorry. I don't answer the door after dark. You never know who might be there. I'm making a pot of tea, would you like a cup?"

I didn't like to say that she was in as much potential danger from strangers at the door during the hours of daylight – in fact, probably more so, but I did accept the offer of tea. We went into her neat kitchen, and there, where I'd left it, was my ring. Oh, the relief! I popped it straight back onto my finger, and gave it a little kiss.

I stayed to have two cups of tea, which I rather regretted half-an-hour later when I left and I was walking up Brindlehurst Avenue heading for the main road and home, a good fifteen to twenty minute walk away, and I suddenly realised I needed a loo. I also realised, as the rain started again, that I'd left Harry's umbrella on the bus.

I dithered a bit. What to do – about a loo *and* the umbrella? Going back to Miss Catesby was out of the question, I wasn't going through all that knocking and shouting again. Would the church hall still be open perhaps? I doubted it, concluded that I might as well head for home. There was little I could do about the brolly, beyond hoping that Joe might find it and hand it in at lost property at the bus station. I reached the junction with Leawood Avenue and saw, a few houses down, a host of blue flashing lights and a small crowd of people. Two police constables in uniform were shooing everyone back as a white Jaguar car pulled up and two men got out.

One was my uncle. The other, the driver, was Laurie.

8

INTERLUDE - DS LAURIE WALKER

Murder is never a pretty sight. My guvnor, DCI Tobias Christopher, has said, several times, that even when you've seen many a dead body, you still do not get used to the horror that one human being can deliberately inflict on another.

"Who is he?" DCI Christopher asked the attending constable who promptly opened his notebook to read out what information he had so far.

"A Mr Duffield. His twin brother found him, he's inside, quite shocked."

The elderly man had been dead about two hours, or so the pathologist thought as an initial experienced guess. I won't go into detail, these things are often a bit grizzly. In this instance there was not much blood, which was a blessing I suppose. The constable, who had been the first to arrive at the scene, had thought quickly and begged umbrellas from the neighbours in a small attempt to keep things dry and preserve what could be preserved of the crime scene.

The old boy lay on his back on the front garden path near the front door, which with all the coming and going, was open. Had it been open earlier when the old boy had been killed? I made a note in my notebook as a reminder to ask.

Jack Carlton, the pathologist, was kneeling beside the victim. He looked up and saw DCI Christopher and me.

"Evening Toby, Laurie. Screwdriver, thrust directly upward into the heart. Either someone who knew what they were doing, or a lucky guess. He'd have lost consciousness from shock within ten or fifteen seconds, brain dead a few minutes later. Final death in about five to eight minutes. He wouldn't have stood a chance, even if he had been found straight away. Not much blood, the weapon is acting as a plug. I'll be able to tell you more when I take a proper look."

"Anything useful on the screwdriver?" I asked.

"Same answer re: knowing more later."

"As soon as possible, maybe?" DCI Christopher said. He never openly pushed anyone to hurry, but his polite asking substantially conveyed his meaning.

"A planned homicide or an accident?" I wondered aloud.

The DCI studied the corpse and the garden, turned slightly to look at the front door about two yards away. "Well, he came to the door for some reason and came out here, so someone had either knocked and he answered, or someone was leaving and he followed them outside. We'll need to know of any callers. House to house, I think, and maybe a public appeal for information, although with the rain I doubt many people were hanging around this afternoon."

Murder was a definite then – although possibly manslaughter, a murder by accident. An intention to threaten or injure, not necessarily meant to kill? Good luck? Hmm, *bad* luck, to hit the heart straight off. Could Duffield have been holding the screwdriver, then slipped and fallen? Not likely. Why would he be out in the front garden in the rain, holding a screwdriver in such a way that if he fell, he'd stab himself?

"Suicide?" I suggested.

The DCI instantly ruled that out. "Unlikely, don't you think? Best check for a note, just in case. We'll need the forensic report to confirm or contradict assumptions."

Leaving Jack to do what he needed to do, and to start seeing to the removal of the body, the DCI suggested, "You have a word with the immediate neighbours, Walker." He pointed to the open front door. "I'll be inside."

I nodded and was heading for the left-hand neighbour's gate when I saw a young lady pushing her way through to the front of the small crowd, which was being encouraged to stand back by a rather soggy police constable. She was waving frantically at me and hopping up and down.

"Jan!" I called, surprised, as I went up to her. "What are you doing here?"

"I could ask the same of you, Laurie. What's happening? Is that the Duffield's house? Is one of them hurt?"

I shook my head. "I'm afraid Mr Duffield is dead."

She looked shocked, her lovely face paling beneath the illumination of the nearest streetlight.

"Oh, Laurie, no! I was here bringing their books only a few hours ago. Was it a heart attack or something? And which one has died, George or Gerald? They are identical twins."

I had to admit that as I'd only just arrived I did not know. I then said, as gently as I could, "As you were here recently, we will need to ask you some questions."

She turned even paler and put her hand over her mouth, her eyes widening.

From behind her shielding fingers she cried,

"Laurie! That means not a natural death, doesn't it? Are you suspecting murder?"

I nodded. "I'm afraid so. You might have been the last but one to see the poor old boy alive."

"Oh Laurie," she repeated, devastated. "The pair of them could be difficult in their own ways... but murder? I'll do whatever I can to help, of course." Then did a sort of little dance, changing from foot to foot. "But I do, desperately, need to visit a loo first."

9

QUESTIONS WITHOUT ANSWERS

Feeling more comfortable, after Laurie obtained permission from my uncle for me to nip into George Duffield's downstairs loo, which had once been a large cupboard next to the front door, I went into the back room where my uncle was standing in front of the sofa where George Duffield was sitting.

I know I shouldn't have been, but I was relieved to see that it was George who was alive, not Gerald. I'm not sure that I could have found it in me to genuinely offer comfort to Gerald. George was in considerable distress. Tears had streaked his poor old wrinkled face and his hands were shaking. Monty was curled on his lap. George looked up when he saw me, he frowned, puzzled, and ushering Monty to the floor, made to stand up but I hurried forward and knelt down in front of him, taking his hands in mine. They were cold, I started to rub some warmth into his stiff, arthritic fingers.

"I've already got my books," he began, his voice shaking as much as his hands. "You came earlier..."

I smiled and said, loudly, "I know, and because I was here, I might be able to help with the police enquiries. DCI Christopher, here, is my uncle. His Sergeant, DS Laurie Walker, is my fiancé." I held out my hand and showed him my ring. "Do you remember, I told you I'd got engaged at New Year?"

George smiled and squeezed my hand. "Yes, yes I remember." He looked up at my uncle standing not far behind me. "She's a lovely girl, Mr Christopher."

"That she is," my uncle agreed as he brought a chair over from the small half-moon dining table for me to sit on, then brought another for himself. "Do you think you could tell me what happened, George?"

George looked confused and bewildered.

"Take your time," I said, rubbing his cold fingers again. I gave a little prompt. "You were in the garden when I left here?"

"Yes. Yes, I was. I was in my greenhouse," he stammered. A few fresh tears trickled down his frail old, whiskery cheeks. "I was checking on my geraniums. Keep them indoors for the winter, see, they don't like the frosty cold. I've some hyacinths ready to break out, too. I'll be bringing them indoors soon. They smell lovely, they do, of a morning when I get up and come in here. Fair fill the air with their perfume. Another few weeks and they'll start to shoot up. Daffs smell nice as well, but it's too early for daffs. I've several in pots. And tulips. I like tulips. Did you know that tulip bulbs were once far more valuable than gold?"

"Any idea of what time you left your greenhouse?" Uncle Toby asked, tactfully getting back to the important subject.

George shook his head.

"You went out into the garden after you'd chosen your books," I said. "That was about three. I watched you from upstairs."

"How long did you stay out there?" my uncle queried.

Again, George shook his head. He didn't know that either.

"He was still outside when I left," I said. "Ten past three, perhaps?"

"I came in because it was starting to rain again and getting gloomy, dusk falls so early this time of year," George said. "I came in, put the kettle on to make myself a cup of tea and feed Monty, my cat. He loves his Kit-E-Kat, but he can be a bit greedy, so I feed him little and often. Mm, little and often. Keeps him happy, see? I put his saucer down and then realised the front door was open – it was cold, a wind blowing through." He patted my hand, apologised. "I'm so sorry my dear, I thought perhaps you'd not closed it properly behind you. So I went to close it and saw..." he gulped, took a few steadying breaths. "Saw, saw my brother."

"Have you any idea why he was out in the front garden? Did he answer a knock at the door, perhaps? Were you expecting anyone?" Uncle asked.

George shook his head. "I was only expecting Miss Christopher. The home help comes on Wednesday and Friday mornings, brings our shopping, does the vacuuming, changes the bed sheets. Milkman leaves milk early, and the postie comes at about eight and then about one if we have anything for a second post, that is. I don't. Gerald does." George faltered. "Usually *did*. He's always writing letters of complaint about this that and the other. *Was* always writing letters. Oh dear..." He paused, then bravely carried on. "We don't get many other callers. Only him, next door regularly complaining. He's always knocking on the wall or the front door, complaining. He's as bad as my brother."

"Meals on Wheels?" I suggested. "Do they deliver?"

"No. Him upstairs won't have them, and I enjoy

cooking for myself. Simple stuff, beans on toast, an omelette, pork chop and mashed spuds. That sort of thing. No idea what he does for himself. *Did* for himself."

"So would he have answered the door?" Uncle asked again. "If someone had knocked?"

I replied for George. "Gerald Duffield rarely came downstairs. He has – had..." I gulped. I was getting my tenses muddled, too. Past tense. *Had* not *has*. "He had a heart condition, so stairs were not easy for him, he got breathless. That's why I deliver books. He only came down if he *really* had to. Plus, the two men didn't get on, avoided each other as much as possible."

Uncle Toby nodded. Said to George, "So you usually answer the door?"

George agreed. "Yes, now that I can hear the bell." He pointed at a large bell on the wall above his television. "My cousin's youngest son set that up not long ago. I'm a bit deaf, you see. When anyone comes the doorbell now rings in here."

"Would your brother have heard it?" Uncle asked.

George answered truthfully, "I wouldn't know, but I think the normal bell is rigged to sound upstairs."

The large doorbell was a good system, as long as George was in his sitting room. I added, "Most of the regular callers, myself, the home help, know there is a key on a string just inside the letter box. We often let ourselves in if George doesn't answer."

Uncle Toby frowned disapproval. I could see by his expression that his thought was something like, *A key on a string is not a good, safe, idea.* I agreed with him, but it was a tried and tested habit for George's generation. Up until the War, and during the fifties, everyone kept a key on a string, or under a flowerpot or on the door lintel. I think it was regarded as safe for ordinary people – there were not many burglaries because there was nothing of value worth stealing. With the coming of the sixties and seventies things were starting to change. Not for the better, unfortunately.

I looked around the room. The library books were piled as I'd left them; nothing else seemed to be disturbed, missing, or out of place. There was one thing that was unusual though. The TV volume was turned right down to low.

"When you came in from the garden, George, did you turn the telly down?" I asked, pointing to it. "Or perhaps you did it when you called the police?" I looked at my uncle, realised that I wasn't sure if George *had* a telephone to call anyone. I looked around, I couldn't see one, and there wasn't one in the hall. "Was it George who called the police?"

"I'll ask DS Walker," he said. "He'll have a note of it."

Despite myself, and the seriousness of the situation, I had to grin. To his face, while at work, my uncle always called Laurie by his surname, 'Walker', or plain 'Sergeant'. At home, or privately, it was Laurie. I supressed a giggle. At our wedding, I suddenly wondered, as 'father' of the bride, would Uncle Toby call his adopted daughter's new husband Walker or Laurie?

George was staring at the flickering black and white screen, puzzled. Shook his head. "Why would I turn the telly down? I can't hear it now." He wiped his face with his wrinkled old hand, took a breath. "I went straight from the kitchen to shut the front door... but..." His voice choked and his words trailed off.

He had found his brother lying dead. They had always professed to dislike each other, but this poor, poor, old man was sitting here, lost and utterly bereft. Perhaps the dislike was not as deep as both of them had made out? Or perhaps...? I shocked myself by thinking it, but perhaps there was another reason for the distress? But surely – *surely* – the dislike hadn't been *that* bad? Bad enough to murder your own brother?

I looked at my uncle, and I could see by his expression that he was having the same suspicious thoughts.

"The TV?" he asked me. "Significant?"

"It's nearly always on. Very loud. It was on at full blast when I left," I explained. "Gerald, upstairs, and Mr Norton next door, get quite cross about it."

I paused, licked my lips uncomfortably. I had used present tense again. "Gerald, Mr Duffield senior, *did* get cross about it. He often had to come downstairs to turn the TV off, which was hard for him to do, but I think sometimes both of them did things to be awkward and deliberately annoying." I covered my mouth with my hand, my eyes widening with embarrassment. "Is that a nasty thing to say?"

"If it is the truth, Jan, then it is best to tell it. Nasty or not. About the living or the dead. Who knows what will, or will not, help us to find who did this?" My uncle cocked his head to one side, raised an eyebrow. "The TV?"

"Oh. Oh yes, well, the volume is so low now, we can't hear it. So someone turned it down. One of your constables perhaps? Or if it was Gerald, then he must have come in here *before* going to the front door."

Poor old George, tears trickling down his face, was sitting in his armchair, stroking Monty, curled on his lap.

I wasn't sure, but did I hear him mutter, "I didn't mean to do it. I really didn't."

10

INTERLUDE - DS LAURIE WALKER

I gathered quite a bit of interesting information from the immediate neighbour to the left of the Duffield's property. Interesting, but not of much help where useful, concrete evidence was needed. Hearsay and personal opinion would never be accepted in a court of law, maybe not even enough to form a charge that would stick. But it sometimes helped us; those tiny comments could fill in a significant gap. I stress, *sometimes*. I know there are many policemen (too many) who have no qualms about fabricating evidence if it leads to a quick, easy, arrest and conviction, but I am not one among them. If a person is proven guilty of a crime, be it theft, murder, rape – or anything in between – then he or she deserves everything that is thrown at them, but an innocent accused of a crime they did not commit all because a policeman couldn't be bothered to do his duty correctly, diligently and honestly? Sorry, that's not in my book. That's why I so enjoy working alongside DCI Christopher. He's not just *good* at his job, he's conscientious at it. I shudder to think how many innocents went to the gallows in error, and all because of incompetency. Black men, foreigners, homosexuals, women. Too many had fallen victim to prejudice, misogyny and corruption.

The neighbour had not made much contact with the deceased, 'Miserable fellow' that he apparently had been.

"Always moaning," the lady of the next door house said leaning against the front door frame, her arms folded, a flower-patterned apron covering her ample frame. "Always grumbling at the kiddies, poor mites. They're only playing, not doing any harm and they're in our own garden. If they can't let off steam there, where can they? Not that I want to speak ill of the dead, of course, and this is shocking, absolutely shocking, but I reckon there's many a person round here who'll not be sad to see Gerald Duffield gone. George now, ah, he's a decent bloke. He's often out in the garden, talks to the kids, happy to toss a ball back if it goes over the fence. As deaf as a post, mind you, but kind-hearted enough. The two of them didn't get on. I often heard Gerald shouting at George, belittling him, bossing him about. Between you and me..." she'd lowered her voice and leant forward at this point, "I wouldn't blame poor old George for losing his patience." At that she'd nodded knowingly, figuratively clamped her lips together and told me she had to get on with cooking the kids' tea. But just before closing the door she had added, "You want to speak to Mr Norton on the other side an' all. Mark my words, he's got a few questions to answer. He complains as much as Gerald did, like World War I it were some days out here between the both of them. The shouting that went on! I wouldn't put a foul deed past that Norton at all. No sir, I wouldn't." And she'd shut the door in my face.

I could well understand the animosity towards Mr Norton. Boy, was he a difficult fellow. Everything he told me was about himself, his unheeded complaints to the council, the police and Uncle Tom Cobley and all. His privacy disturbed, his annoyance at 'their' selfishness. The cat digging up the garden, the noise of the TV. The moment I started to interview him I was itching to put him as our prime suspect.

11

DOWNSTAIRS, UPSTAIRS, AND OUT THE WINDOW

The constable got a bit of a rollocking from my uncle when he admitted touching the TV. A reprimand politely put, but with clear meaning: *Never interfere with a crime scene unless given permission*. Although, knowing how loud George Duffield had his telly, I couldn't blame the constable for turning the sound down. And it did show one thing: Gerald Duffield did not go into his brother's part of the house before he was murdered.

Laurie returned from speaking with the neighbours to each side. He caught my raised eyebrow expression indicating a question, *how did you get on*? and winked at me. I tried not to laugh, disguised my snort as a cough. Which earned me a 'Paddington Bear Hard Stare' from my uncle. I'm convinced that the author, Michael Bond, must have known my uncle and that unsettling, disapproving look of his, and adapted it for his children's stories. Apparently, I can imitate the same look when required.

"Better take a look upstairs," Uncle Toby said, putting his finger to his lips, indicating that Laurie was not to speak in front of George. (Although he would not have been able to hear.) "Come with us, Jan. You might spot something we wouldn't notice."

"So what did you learn?" Uncle Toby asked as we trooped up the stairs.

"The woman next door had nothing much to say," Laurie said, "but didn't like Gerald Duffield, and can't abide Norton. It was he who telephoned the police, by the way. He, or so he maintains, was coming from his house to this one to complain about the volume of the TV, and found George bending over Gerald. He yelled at him to stand back – he was about to remove the murder weapon. Norton was a Pacifist but served as a stretcher-bearer during both wars. He was at Ypres, Passchendaele and the Somme. Come the second lot, he did his bit in the East End of London during the Blitz and then went to Normandy for the landings. He has several prestigious medals, including the George Cross, and knows a good bit about first aid. He said he thought the 'cantankerous old basket'– his words, not mine – had only been dead a few minutes."

"He saw a good bit of action, then?" Uncle Toby said. "Capable of losing his temper and making a silly mistake?"

"As a pacifist, unlikely to murder anyone. But he's got one heck of a lot of temper on him. Which is a huge inconsistency. And we've only got his word about the sequence of events. Unless George has confirmed things?" Laurie queried as we neared the top of the stairs.

Uncle Toby shook his head. "Can't get much from him, he's too shaken to think clearly."

"Norton might have been a pacifist," I said, puffing a little, the stairs were steep, "but he was always excessively curt and rude to me. As was Gerald Duffield. Two of a kind, both of them."

"He wasn't exactly likeable, I agree," Laurie said.

"Dislikes this, that and everything under the sun, including – no especially – the police." He glanced over his shoulder at me. "Had a good word to say about you though, Jan. Said how you were always cheerful and brought him good books to read."

" Oh, the hypocritical old cabbage!" I exclaimed. "He constantly moans at me."

"Moans about his neighbours as well. I quote: 'All those bang, bang, bang, westerns and whooping Indians.' He said he asked you to tell his neighbour to turn the TV down, Jan? Said it went quiet for a bit then started up again."

I frowned. "He did mention the TV. He knew I would be coming here next, but George always turns the telly off when I'm here. Turns it back on as soon as I leave."

"Perhaps," Uncle Toby offered, being as fair minded as he always tried to be, "perhaps Norton is somewhat curt and doesn't like the noise because of his wartime experiences? If I'd have been in the thick of dealing with the injured, dead and dying in just *one* of those dreadful places during either of the wars, I doubt I would be able to guarantee a congenial temper."

I grinned at him. "So what's your excuse for being an occasional grump? You were safe from the war deciphering codes and such in deepest, darkest Buckinghamshire."

"Safe from Hitler, yes," he said with a perfectly serious face, "but not safe from the clutches of a certain determined young lady." He laughed. "Your aunt was as much of a force to be reckoned with back then as she is now."

From the landing I indicated Gerald's bedroom at the front of the house and the living room at the back.

"Do you remember seeing anyone else loitering around outside?" Uncle Toby asked as we entered the boxroom kitchen. It was a bit of a squash, so I stayed at the door.

I had already been thinking about seeing anyone, so could answer immediately. "No, no one. My driver did pop back to check he'd locked the van up – we'd stopped for a cup of tea and a cake at the church hall. He was about fifteen, twenty minutes, perhaps? He might have seen someone."

"That seems quite a while to nip back, lock up, then return to the church hall?" Laurie remarked.

"He said that he had to stop for a pee," I added. "Used the bushes beside the Baptist Church – oh, he said there was a lady locking up, so he had to keep hidden."

"You'd better interview him tomorrow," Uncle said to Laurie, who nodded, his hand on the Russell Hobbs electric kettle.

"I'll call in at the depot first thing. Kettle's quite cold."

"He'll not be there," I interrupted. "He's gone off to the Isle of Wight, fishing."

Laurie grimaced. "I'll track this church lady down instead. Maybe see if Hampshire Police can find our driver and interview him? Or would you like me to go and find him?"

"We'll see how we go," Uncle answered.

Everything was neat and tidy in the kitchen, lunchtime dishes drying on a rack beside a small sink. Several items of food in a small refrigerator: cheese, bacon, a pork pie. Milk, eggs. We went into the living room, again all neat and tidy. Uncle Toby and Laurie searched through a few drawers, looked inside the wooden roll-top desk in the corner.

"We'll need to have a proper look at all this paperwork later," Laurie said, indicating the various cubbyholes inside the desk. "I'll get the team onto it."

I couldn't see anything different from when I had been here earlier. The book about King Charles I was on the arm of the only comfortable chair, open on the second page. He'd started to read it, then.

We went into the bedroom, although I was of no help here because Gerald always kept the door closed so I had never seen inside. I went to the window, drew the net curtain back and peered out. It was quite dark now, the lit street lamps glistened on the wet pavement and reflected in the puddles. I could see cars passing along the main road at the top of the slight rise at the end of Leawood Avenue. That bit at the top was always dark as there were no houses, just the back garden of the corner house on the main road, and opposite it, the white-walled Baptist Church. I could just about see the orangey-yellow flash of the Belisha beacon winking on and off at the zebra crossing. A few pedestrians, two walking up towards the main road, one coming down the other way with an umbrella dipped against the driving rain. He turned into Brindlehurst Avenue and I lost sight of him. There were a few people hanging round outside the Duffields' house, eager to watch what was going on. Several, I guessed, were reporters. Nearly all of them held umbrellas.

"Rubbing salt into my wound," I muttered.

"What's that?" Uncle Toby asked, overhearing.

I explained about leaving Harry's umbrella on the bus.

"I expect the conductor would have handed it into lost property at the terminus," Laurie suggested. "We can call in later and ask, perhaps?"

"They'll be closed," Uncle Toby pointed out.

Resigned, I shrugged. "No matter, I can go tomorrow. It's Wednesday, my day off."

"Might need you to come to the police station to make a formal statement?" Uncle said. He often termed important things as if they were a mild question, it made it sound less officious I think.

"I'll go to the stables and do the horses with Aunt Madge in the morning, then call in to see you? Will that be all right?" I asked.

He nodded.

"Oh heck," I added. "I forgot, I offered to exercise one of the ponies, a little black monster. The young girl who rides him has been ill these past weeks and the pony hasn't been ridden much. I said I'd take him out."

"It won't take all morning though, will it?" Laurie queried.

"No, a canter across Chingford Plains and a good trot along the sandy rides will wear him out."

"See you in the afternoon then?"

It seemed to be a day for forgetting things. It was only as I was snug in bed, dozing off, that I remembered I hadn't mentioned about the man Mrs Colchester had seen. I didn't worry too much. The poor man was probably totally innocent of her suspicions. I also hadn't told my uncle about hearing George Duffield muttering that he 'shouldn't have done it'. Now that *was* important. But did I have it in my heart to say anything?

12

PONY PRANKS

Mullet looked like the shaggy pony in the Thelwell cartoons – even his name was similar (the Thelwell pony was called 'Kipper'). At just under fourteen hands high – although that could easily also be his waist measurement – he was a Pony With Attitude. *His* attitude, that is. His owner, Lottie, had been poorly with German measles for several weeks (thankfully much better for Christmas) so, what with feeling poorly and the festive season, she hadn't been to the yard for a while, but wanted to start riding again. For the past several weeks Mullet had enjoyed the freedom of grazing in the field; now it was time to return to earning his keep and doing some work. Lottie was only nine years old and her mum thought it would be sensible to have the pony exercised a few times by someone with more ability, as he could be a bit 'determined'. There were a couple of capable lightweight ladies up the yard who could ride him, and although I wasn't as lightweight as they were, I was well within the weight he could carry. (I thought I was plump, especially after the fabulous Christmas food I'd put away, but Laurie maintained that I was 'suitably cuddly'. Which, I had pointed out, also perfectly described my teddy bear.)

"Are you sure you want to take Mullet out?" Aunt Madge queried as she tacked up one of her own horses, Kaler.

"Yes, if we do a quick circuit it should be enough to let most of the wind out of his sails for Lottie to ride him after school."

What's the saying? Famous last words?

We were fine riding side by side down the drive and along the road, Madge towering above me on 16 hand Kaler, Mullet walking along nicely with what I was soon to realise was a 'butter wouldn't melt' expression.

We turned off the road and trotted along the sandy ride that ran parallel. So far, all well and good. Coming out from beneath the shadow of the bare-branched trees we trotted onto the wide open Chingford Plains. This was an expanse of grassland steeped in history. Up on the crest of the hill on the far side was an ancient building, the Queen Elizabeth Hunting Lodge – that's Elizabeth I not the present Queen Elizabeth II. Good Queen Bess used to regularly hunt in the Royal Forest of Epping, and I assume, stay overnight or at least take luncheon in the hunting lodge. It is said that on hearing England's victory of the Armada she was so overjoyed she rode her horse into the building and straight up the grand oak staircase. (I wonder how they got the animal down again?)

On one part of the Plains you could see where farmers used the common land for arable farming, the undulating hollows of furrows were still there. I'm not sure if this was from the period of Enclosures, when ruthless landowners confiscated common grazing land, or during the two Wars when every bit of land was needed for growing food. I'll look it up and find out one day, when I have a bit of spare time.

The nice thing about the Plains for horse riders were the designated bridle paths, which gave an ideal space to have a good blast. Aunt Madge and I set off together at a steady canter – not too fast, although in good weather a gallop can be tempting, but after the rain the ground was muddy and slippy. About fifty yards across, Mullet decided he'd had enough exercise. He put his head down and bucked three times in quick succession. Now, I'm a good rider and he is only a pony, but even with clamping my legs round his rotund body I didn't stand a chance. I was off, sailing through the air to land in a heap in the mud. I clung onto the reins but the bridle was too big for him and it slid straight off over his head. Next thing, he sort of wiggled (I kid ye not – Aunt Madge is a witness), he wiggled and wriggled and in two shakes of a pony's tail got the saddle off as well! I have never seen a pony do that before. So, riderless, bridle and saddle-less he kicked up his heels and sprinted off in the direction of home, Aunt Madge following after him.

"Stay where you are!" she yelled, "I'll be back as soon as I can."

Fortunately, a lovely couple were walking their dog and saw everything that had happened. (Two more witnesses to back me up.) They came over to see if I needed help.

I did. Winded and feeling mighty foolish I sat there wondering if I was going to be sick.

My arm hurt. Hurt like heck.

13

CASUALTY

Whipps Cross hospital had wonderful staff but it was an old building completed in 1903. For some of the corridors you could be forgiven for thinking that date ought to be 1803. In the main corridor there was a brass plaque which somewhat summed the place up:

This tablet was erected to commemorate the visit of
Their Majesties King George V & Queen Mary with H.R.H. Princess Mary,
to this Infirmary and War Hospital on Saturday, 17 November 1917,
when Their Majesties visited the wounded soldiers and the Queen presented
the medals and certificates of training to the nurses.

I must confess, I had no idea who 'Princess Mary' was, nor was I interested in the history of the building, or any brass plaques, however royal, on this particular visit because my left arm was broken. Well, cracked. The initial X-ray wasn't clear as my hand and arm had puffed up like a balloon, so I was given a supportive sling and told to come back in a few days to get re-Xrayed and probably plastered. Naturally, I made the predictable corny gag about "I'll use my aunt's gin!" which earned me a filthy look from the prim nurse who, I swear, was a replica of Hattie Jaques as the stern matron in the *Carry On* films.

The biggest upset: I'd had to remove my ring. Aunt Madge had more-or-less thrown her horse and the wretched pony, who had arrived safe and unharmed back at the yard, to her groom (more of a part-time helper really, but 'groom' sounded more professional), scrambled into her car and broken the speed limit to get back to me. I'd insisted that I was all right, but my arm was already swelling, and she had insisted that I must remove my ring. I made her *swear* that she would put it in a safe place. She slid it onto one of her fingers and *promised* to pop it into her handbag, which was in the car.

"If you don't take it off now, and your arm swells even more than it already has, the hospital will have to cut it off," she said as she fashioned a sling from her silk scarf.

"What! My arm?" I squeaked in alarm.

That made her laugh, which was good because she was quite pale with worry. Apparently, I was even paler, but adrenalin was kicking in and I honestly didn't feel too bad. We thanked the kind Good Samaritans who had stayed with me, and I wobbled to Aunt Madge's car parked nearby in the car park. Needless to say, I had felt fine while sitting on the muddy grass with a blanket round my shoulders, kindly set there by my helpers who'd fetched it from their car. The moment I stood up everything started swimming as shock and dizziness set in.

Once sitting down again I said I was fine, but Aunt M totally ignored me and drove straight to Whipps

Cross Hospital casualty. Hence the frumpy nurse and the brass plaque.

We completely forgot about the umbrella, and I didn't manage to get to the police station to make my statement. Laurie came to me instead, but what with the pain, the shock and the strong painkillers the hospital had given me, I was terribly groggy, so he abandoned the idea.

I will emphasise, however, that the gin joke *was* just a joke.

Aunt Madge chivvied Laurie away, informed me that she would telephone work first thing in the morning to tell them I would be off sick for a while, then tucked me in and told me to go to sleep. I didn't need much telling. I was vaguely aware of Uncle Toby coming into my room to see how I was doing.

I discovered an enormous vase of red roses beside my bed in the morning with a note from Laurie telling me to get well soon and that he loved me. Which was wonderful of him, but didn't stop my arm hurting.

14

TEA AND TOAST

Uncle Toby tiptoed into my room in the early afternoon the next day. Thursday, when he usually had an afternoon off work – essential work permitting, which it usually wasn't. He carried a tray with a steaming mug of tea and a plate piled with hot, buttered toast. He was still wearing his suit, so I guessed he'd not been home long as he usually changed into something more casual and comfortable as soon as he could.

"Hello, Cupcake," he said as he put the tray on my bedside cabinet and sat down on the bed. "Madge has sent this up, says you've been asleep for most of the morning and not eaten much."

I sat up and blearily looked at my clock. Gone 2 p.m. My arm ached. Aunt Madge had strapped it aslant across my chest, which prevented me from moving it about but didn't stop the pain. Uncle Toby stuffed two extra pillows behind my back and I nibbled at the toast, then swapped to holding the tea, which Uncle Toby handed me.

"Feel up to talking?" he asked. "We can leave it until tomorrow if you like, but there's a lot I need to know about the Duffields."

I'm ashamed to say, I'd forgotten all about Gerald and George. But then, I'd had other things on my mind and had swallowed some pretty hefty painkillers.

"Isn't it your afternoon off?" I asked.

He shrugged, "A policeman's lot and all that."

"What do you need to know?" I offered, although my head was as muzzy as a fog-bound damp morning.

"Anything and everything. We've no idea of a motive. Was this killing random or deliberate? Why did Gerald Duffield open the front door, and to whom? We want to start putting a picture together and, so far, we haven't got even a faintly blurred sketch."

"Has George not been able to help?" I said, wolfing another half-slice of toast. I was ravenous.

"He's told us all about the German warplane and the train, and I now know a lot more about TV westerns and the best way to grow tomatoes, but otherwise, no, he's hardly said anything of relevance, outside the fact that the two of them couldn't stand each other."

"Did he say why?" I queried. "It must have been something big and tragic to end up hating your own brother so intensely."

"Lots of siblings don't get on. Usually because of rivalry or money – lack of it, that is. Murder is more likely to be committed by someone known, someone who can get close, act unexpectedly."

I used the excuse of eating toast to remain silent a moment. I didn't remember my own twin sister, June, I was too young when she died, but I have always resented her. Which is ridiculous because I didn't know her and had no reason to be envious of her. I chewed at another piece of toast. Or did I? I do remember my mother always going on about June, what a lovely baby she was; how good she was. I even remember Mum saying, once, in a fit of temper when I'd been naughty about something that the wrong baby had died. I was very young, but I'd understood what she had meant, even if she hadn't *meant* it. Or had she? Mum had been grieving, of course, but all the same... Maybe I did have a grudge? I said none of this to Uncle Toby. He and Aunt Madge had adopted me when Mum had died, and I didn't want him to think that I had any lingering resentments of any sort.

"I get the feeling that there was something to do with the war that caused the rift," I said tentatively. "George was always going on about that incident, the praise and medal he'd received for it. 'I was a hero', he said that quite often. I don't think Gerald did much in the war, if anything. Or if he did, he never gave any sort of counterblast of heroics. All he says is how he regrets not being able to go to Oxford." I paused. I could hear the telephone ringing downstairs. "Might have been Cambridge, I never really listened to him. Not properly." That in itself was sad. The poor man was dead by brutal means and I had never bothered to listen to him when he was alive.

"Whatever the reason, Cupcake, the resentment against each other was bitter. Most people have feelings of guilt or remorse after someone close has died, especially in these sorts of circumstances, but our Mr George Duffield seems only too pleased that his brother has gone."

I gasped, realising what he meant. "Oh goodness! You don't think George did it, do you?"

Uncle did a sort of yes/no nod of his head. "*Mmm hmm.* It's a distinct possibility. We found a box of screwdrivers in the garden shed. Several were missing from the set, which is the same make as the one used. Bought from Woolworths." He mimed holding something clasped in his hand and stabbed it against his chest in the vicinity of his heart. "We think Gerald might have known his killer."

I swallowed hard, told my uncle about the words I'd heard George mutter. Added, "But if George did it, why lure Gerald outside? More opportunities indoors – and plenty of other weapons at hand. A kitchen knife, push him down the stairs, tamper with something electrical..." I was horrified at gentle George being a suspect, even though I had wondered this myself on Tuesday, but before my uncle could say anything more Aunt Madge was calling anxiously up the stairs.

"Toby? Toby, it's the Station. There's been another of those awful burglaries."

Uncle Toby frowned and took the empty plate from me, left me to finish the mug of tea. "No rest for the wicked, it seems." He smiled ruefully and headed off downstairs. He'd left the door open, so I heard him say to my aunt: "Those burglaries are being investigated by DS Fallon. Why call me?"

Although she spoke in a low tone, her troubled reply drifted up the stairs. "This one's different, Toby."

15

FLOWERS ON FRIDAY

Aunt Madge brought me breakfast in bed the next morning – bacon sandwiches oozing with a thick layer of brown HP sauce accompanied by a large mug of steaming hot tea. She sat on the bed and offered to read aloud the headline Chingford Guardian newspaper article – she'd brought the paper along with the breakfast, but realised I couldn't hold it and enjoy the sandwiches at the same time, having only one hand in working order.

"The murder is covered, but not quite accurate," she said, folding the paper in half to read from the front page.

"They got the report in quick. Don't they go to press on Thursday afternoons?"

"I think most of it is put to bed – is that the term? – during Wednesday, but the front page is held until Thursday for any last minute news."

"Which gets missed out if anything interesting happens on a Thursday evening," I laughed. "So what does it say?"

Aunt Madge settled herself on the bed, took a slurp of her own tea and began reading. "It says here: '*Gerald*

Duffield (76) was found dead, under suspicious circumstances, in the front garden of his house in Leawood Avenue on Wednesday afternoon. Led by DCI Tobias Christopher, Chingford CID are investigating and are appealing for any witnesses who were in the vicinity between 5 and 6 p.m. Duffield was a schoolmaster teaching geography at Islecott Grammar School for Boys until he retired at the age of 65.' That's the big school up on the main road isn't it?"

"Hang on," I interrupted, through a mouthful of bacon butty. "Geography? I thought he taught Latin and history."

"It says geography here. Where was I? *'Duffield served as an air raid warden in Stratford for most of the war years, being exempt from National Service due to a heart condition. He leaves behind a twin brother, George, who was decorated with the George Medal during WWII for stopping a train in a Devonshire tunnel, thus saving it from an aggressive attack by a German Messerschmitt. Due to his heroic action only one life was lost.'."*

Aunt Madge tutted and squinted at the paper. "Oh, the rain's dripped here and the ink's smudged, I can't read the next bit. *Something, something, something,* then, *'the funeral has yet to be arranged.'* And that's it."

"Is that the George Cross?" I asked, astonished, and impressed. If so, old George Duffield had every right to boast of his achievement.

"No. The GM was awarded for gallantry in circumstances where military honours were not appropriate. At the height of the Blitz in 1940, there was a need to reward many acts of courage performed by non-military personnel, so the George Cross and the George Medal were initiated to recognise gallantry during enemy bombing and general brave deeds. The military equivalent would, I suppose, be the Victoria Cross and Military Medal. I remember the announcement about it by King George on the radio."

It might sound a bit silly, naïve even, but I often forgot that Uncle Toby and Aunt Madge had been involved in the war –1939 to 1945 war, that is. I think this is because they weren't old. Old as in George and Gerald Duffield, I mean. (Aunt Madge would kill me if I implied that she was 'old', she was only in her mid-forties after all – but that did seem old to me.) "Does the report say anything else about either of them?" I queried, mentally changing my train of thought, if you'll forgive the slight pun about trains.

I think I might have been secretly hoping to have a mention in the article, but there was no reason whatsoever for the Guardian to do so, or even have the information, so I was daft to feel a twinge of disappointment when Aunt Madge scanned down the rest of the short column and found nothing more of much relevance.

"There are a couple of quotes from the school. Tactful, I think. *'He was a dedicated master'* and *'His retirement elicited many best wishes'.*"

"Code for *Thank goodness he's gone*?"

"*Mm*, sounds like it."

"Not surprising that Gerald was miffed about George's story-telling is it? All Gerald did was teach in a boys' school, while his brother got a prestigious medal for driving a train into a tunnel."

Aunt Madge nodded, but corrected my assumption. "There was more to that train driving than you think. Speeds like that were – still are – rare, and it took skill to maintain control while some crazed German was shooting the hell out of you. Plus skilful timing to put the brakes on without tipping the entire train off the tracks. Your Mr George Duffield is well-deserving of his medal."

I saw her point.

"Just a shame," she said, "that Gerald Duffield's somewhat morbid five minutes of fame has come because he was murdered."

Aunt Madge started to look through the rest of the paper to see if there was anything else that might interest me. The front doorbell rang. "Now who can that be?" she said, folding up the paper, and setting it down, picking up my empty plate and mug instead. "You stay put, don't even *think* about getting up."

Needless to say, I ignored her. I felt woozy but that was the painkillers, I'd had enough of them to make me rattle, and I'd had enough of lazing in bed with nothing much to do. I had tried reading but my eyes were fuzzy, and I knew that if I remained where I was I'd only doze off again. I swung my legs out of bed as my bedroom door opened and Laurie walked in. He had a huge bouquet of flowers in his hand.

"How are you feeling... and your aunt said that you have orders to stay in bed."

"I'm fine, but bored. The flowers are lovely, thank you – but you've already brought me some." I pointed to the beautiful roses on my bedside cabinet.

Laurie frowned at the bouquet in his hand. "These aren't from me, I found them on the doorstep." He inspected the cellophane wrapping. "That's odd. No card."

"From the girls at the library perhaps?" I suggested. Although why they'd leave them on the doorstep and not knock, I didn't know.

Aunt Madge came in with a large vase filled with water, took the flowers from Laurie and started arranging them after giving me a stern look and pointing with her finger at the bed. I gave in, and swung my legs back under the covers.

"You can get up this afternoon," she ordered. "I'll

light the fire in the sitting room and you can stretch out on the sofa to watch TV. You're *not* to move from bed until I come back from the stables, is that understood?" She put the vase of flowers on my chest of drawers and cleared away the debris of leaves and stalks. "I'm going up the yard now, just to turn the horses out. The girls are doing the mucking out for me. I won't be long, and you've Laurie here to keep an eye on you for a while." She waltzed to the door, disappeared out onto the landing then popped her head back round the door. She was grinning. "And no doing anything I wouldn't do," she laughed.

"I don't know what you mean!" Laurie feigned indignation, then laughed and leant forward and gave me a resounding kiss – being careful of my arm.

"Aren't you supposed to be at work?" I asked, cocking my head to one side to look at him. He was handsome (I know, I'm biased), but he did look like a young Cary Grant, and you couldn't get much handsomer than that.

He looked a bit sheepish and fiddled with the buttons of his jacket. "Well, you see," he stammered, "I'm actually here on official business." He stopped fiddling with the buttons and took out his notebook and pencil from his pocket.

"This is official, is it?" I said with a smile. "Although I don't think I can tell you any more about George or Gerald Duffield. Uncle Toby said you suspect George of murdering his brother. Surely not?" Although, there were those words he'd muttered...

Laurie shook his head. "No, we haven't any evidence against George. Let's just say at this stage he continues to help us with our enquiries."

I was a little startled. "Oh! You haven't arrested him have you? Poor George."

Laurie laughed. "No, he's safe and comfortable at

home. We have interviewed him, and there are one or two inconsistencies, but he's elderly, deaf, and bewildered. We checked about what you said you'd heard him say. He answered that he was talking to that cat, apologising for locking him in a cupboard?"

Laurie had framed it as a question. I nodded confirmation. "Yes, the cupboard under the stairs. I let poor Monty out."

Laurie shrugged. "Could be genuine, then. There again... Anyway, a cousin and her son have come to stay with the old boy for a bit. Help him sort things out."

"Keep an eye on him, you mean? Make sure he doesn't leave the country?"

"Keep an eye for his own sake, yes – he's quite shaken up. But leave the country? I think that belongs more to TV cop shows. Most ordinary people don't even hold a passport."

I couldn't argue with that as I didn't have one. I did try though, "But most ordinary people don't commit murder, do they? Maybe it's the *unordinary* people you need to look out for?" I wriggled a bit more comfortably into the pillows that Aunt Madge had propped behind me before I'd started eating. "So what do you need to know?"

Laurie sat on the bed. (Most unorthodox for an official visit by a policeman.) He took hold of my uninjured hand. (Also unorthodox.) "I'm afraid this isn't good news, Jan love."

Suddenly, I felt frightened. "What is it?" I whispered. "Has something happened to Uncle Toby?"

Laurie smiled, his thumb stroking my fingers. "I don't think your aunt would be so calm or talking about doing her horses if that were the case! DCI Christopher is fine, at least he was about twenty minutes ago when I left him arguing with a worn typewriter ribbon."

"So what is it? Tell me."

He took a moment to gather his thoughts. "You delivered books to a Miss Mary Catesby on Tuesday?"

For one awful moment I thought he knew about my carelessness with my engagement ring. I ought to have told him straight away, had meant to say something yesterday, but naughty ponies and broken arms sort of distracted me.

I nodded. "Yes, she's lovely. My best customer."

Laurie took another steadying breath. "I'm afraid she was burgled on Tuesday evening, we think by the same person who's been doing this spate of thefts, although this one was a different M.O. so might not be."

I was horrified. "Oh no! She's an absolute sweetie. How dare this person do something so despicable?"

When he didn't answer I instinctively knew there was something else.

"There's more to it, Jan. She was viciously attacked. Her right cheekbone and eye socket broken. He – or she, though we suspect a he – struck her quite forcefully on the face with something solid, we don't know what. Her Meals on Wheels lady found her on the floor of her hall yesterday lunchtime."

"Laurie, how awful! But yesterday was Thursday. You said she was burgled on Tuesday?"

He nodded. "When Meals on Wheels didn't get an answer on Wednesday they assumed Miss Catesby was out..."

I blurted, "She never goes out, apart from Tuesday lunchtime."

"It was a relief delivery on Wednesday. The normal M.O.W. lady on Thursday realised there was something wrong. When they looked closer they saw Miss Catesby on the floor and broke in."

"You mean she'd been lying there, brutally injured, for hours? Oh, poor, poor Miss Catesby. Where is she? In hospital? I must go and see her..." I started trying to push him aside in an attempt to get up. Gently, he restrained me.

"Stay where you are, love, there's nothing you can do. She'd been there since Tuesday evening."

Then it hit me. That telephone call yesterday lunchtime. Laurie and Uncle Toby were detectives already working on a murder case. There was another team looking into these burglaries. I could feel the colour draining from my face and tears starting to swell. Only another murder would involve my uncle and my fiancé.

"Oh Laurie," I whispered, choking back a sob. "She's dead, isn't she?"

I gave up trying to hold back the tears when he nodded.

16

A FRIGHT

I watched TV in the afternoon, although there was not anything particular on. I did enjoy Bernard Cribbins reading *The Emperor's New Clothes* on Children's Jackanory, I loved the way he put on different voices and really drew you into the tales he read. Aunt Madge had gone back up to the yard to feed the horses their tea, and it was already dark outside – dreary January days with early dark nights, not helped along by rainy drizzle all day. Roll on summer. I managed to throw another log on the open fire – we had central heating, but it was so much cosier with the fire lit and apple and ash logs burning. Basil, Aunt Madge's rogue of a black cat, was curled on the rug in front of the fire; he woke up and scowled at me as I clumsily hefted a log from basket to fire. I say 'hefted' – it wasn't actually a big log but one-handed it was awkward to manoeuvre. I was wondering whether to lob on a second log when I heard a rattle at the front door letterbox.

"Postman? This time in the afternoon?" I said to Basil, who completely ignored me. I went to the window and pulled aside the blue velvet curtain to peer out. There was no one in the front garden – more of a rectangular paved area, where we parked the cars, with hedging and low-growing shrubs along each of the borders. The wrought-iron double gates were open, as they would be when Aunt Madge was out in her car. Laurie's old Morris Minor was parked by the hedge, where he left it every morning when he arrived to collect Uncle Toby – swapping his old thing for my uncle's white Jaguar. A bus was stopped at the bus stop. As I watched, it trundled off. A woman was hurrying by, her head tucked under a bright red umbrella, a Great Dane on a lead pulling her along. I recognised her as our next-door-but-one neighbour. No one else was in view.

I went out into the hall and found an envelope on the doormat. Addressed to me. I went back to my cosy chair and evicted Basil who had taken advantage of those few minutes to jump into my spot. Cheeky monkey. "Jump into my grave as quick, would you?" I admonished with a laugh.

The envelope felt a bit flimsy for a get well card, but tucking it under my chin I managed to tear the envelope open, then clamped one corner between my teeth while I extracted the folded piece of paper from inside.

Hello. Did you like my flowers?
Was that your boyfriend with you?
I don't like him. He'll have to go.
All my love

I stared at the note for quite a while, a chill crawling up my spine, despite the blaze of warmth from the fire. The flowers that had been left on the doorstep without a card to say who they were from? Who was this person? A secret admirer? But if so, one who sounded exceedingly creepy. How dare he say he didn't like my Laurie – and what did *He'll have to go* mean?

Disgusted, I made to throw the note on the fire, then thought better of it and propped it, and the envelope, on the mantlepiece. I went back to the window, peered out from behind the curtain again. It was even darker now, the rain heavier. Headlights from the passing traffic lit up the falling rain and reflected on the road. No sign of Aunt Madge yet. Uncle Toby would not be back home until late, as he and Laurie were working on the two murder cases. I went to the front door and hooked the safety chain into place, then checked all the doors and windows to ensure they were locked. I don't know why I felt so uneasy, but the hairs on the back of my neck were prickling.

I found my hand hovering over the telephone receiver in the hall. Shall I phone my uncle? Then nearly jumped out of my skin as a car's headlights swept in through the open gates and poured in through the glass window in the front door. I stood there frozen. I stupidly stood there, tears streaming down my face as I recognised the Jaguar and saw Laurie step out from the driver's side.

"It's nothing to be scared of," Laurie said, having read the note through twice – holding it carefully by the corners. "I mean, it isn't threatening or anything, is it?"

I disagreed. "It says he doesn't like you and you've got to go."

Laurie laughed as he moved to put his arm round me. "If I had a pound note for every time someone said they didn't like me, I'd be rich by now. Look, I'll keep this safe, take it into Chingford Police Station – I might be able to get someone to fingerprint it, but I doubt it. We're a tad busy at the moment."

"I'm just being silly," I admitted. "Probably because I was all on my own, and my arm hurts. Could you run upstairs and get those flowers for me, dump them in the bin? I don't want them."

Laurie pulled a face. "No point in keeping them if you don't want them, and I haven't time to trawl round the florists to see if they happen to recognise anything – unlikely, they're common florist's flowers. Seems a waste to bin them, though. Tell you what; I'll stash them in the boot of my car, and drop them off at the cemetery tomorrow morning – put them on the first grave I come to that hasn't got any flowers."

I liked that idea.

"Now, I came for a reason, Jan."

I pretended a pout. "Oh. Not to see me?"

"Of course, to see you." He kissed the tip of my nose. "But we wondered if you would mind taking a look round Miss Catesby's house to see if there's anything missing. No one else seems to have been inside much."

I wasn't too keen on the idea. "Not her luncheon friend or the neighbour?"

He puffed his cheeks. "Not discovered who the friend is yet, the neighbour rarely went beyond the front door, and the Meals on Wheels lady only went into the kitchen."

"I didn't go anywhere else either, only her kitchen and lounge."

"But you knew her, so would you mind coming? We could do with some help," Laurie coaxed.

I was tired and still shaken, but I reluctantly agreed – if he would go upstairs to fetch my shoes and those flowers, and leave a note for Aunt Madge.

"You can explain to her," I insisted, "why I'm not sitting in front of the fire doing nothing except watching TV and dozing."

I had a feeling that she would be furious, so Laurie could shoulder the blame.

17

AN EMPTY HOUSE

This was the second house this week that I'd walked into in order to look at a dead person's things. It was starting to become a habit, one that I did not enjoy. I'd not felt emotional in Gerald Duffield's flat because I didn't like him, and the place had felt impersonal, almost alien. It had never had a cosy, welcoming feel to it – neither did George's downstairs flat, come to that, but upstairs had felt hostile and resentful, downstairs was always... indifferent. Yes, that's the right word. Indifferent.

Miss Catesby's house, by contrast, had always been pleasantly friendly, but now it was cold and uninviting. No cheerful fire blazing in the sitting room, no kettle singing, almost on the boil, on the gas stove in the kitchen. There was a heavy presence of *nothing* in the house. It felt empty of life, warmth and welcome. I stood in the hall, just beyond the front door. The taxidermy puffin was in bits on the carpet, the glass case smashed to pieces, the bird itself now headless, with feathers scattered everywhere. Poor thing, having to suffer indignity twice over. Near the first open doorway to the large lounge, a chalk outline of a body marked where Miss Catesby had lain injured, and subsequently died. The pathologist, Laurie had told me, said that she'd passed away during that first Tuesday night when the temperature had dropped. The only comfort: he didn't think that she had regained consciousness.

I felt the un-presence of her wash over me like a smothering wave. I'd been caught by a huge wave at the seaside once when I was about four years old. I'd never forgotten it and never felt comfortable paddling in the sea since. I was splashing in the shallows, dressed, but barefoot. I remember laughing at Aunt Madge a yard or so away as she hopped about wailing that the water was cold. Then I'd tripped over, falling backwards, and sat there in the wet sand, slow to register that my aunt was now shouting at me to get up – and an enormous wave had engulfed me. I recall staying there as it receded, soaked to the bone, still sitting there, everything dripping, totally stunned and breathless. Then I'd tipped my head back and let out an enormous shriek of cold, wet, indignation. Looking back, the incident was funny, although it wasn't at the time. A similar shriek, but this one of grief, was building inside me as I stood there in Miss Catesby's empty hall.

Noticing that I was shaking, Laurie put his arms around me and held me tight, mindful of my arm, his hand gently stroking my hair while I wept.

Somewhere nearby, my uncle said, "Is she all right? Perhaps this wasn't advisable?"

That brought me back to my senses, strengthened my resolve. I pushed Laurie away and fumbled for a handkerchief to wipe my eyes and blow my nose. He passed me his.

"It's just silly emotion," I apologised, sniffing. "She was such a lovely lady."

"Nothing to apologise for where caring for others is concerned, Cupcake," said my uncle coming into the hall from the second door into the through-lounge – the front and back rooms had been knocked into one, it was the reason Miss Catesby had bought the house, or so she'd told me. *Nice and light and airy, and I can see out to the back and the front at the same time.*

I took a deep breath and pulled myself together. I had a job to do here, and for her sake I wanted to do it properly. "Right then," I said, taking a second breath. "You said you have several sets of fingerprints? Miss Catesby's naturally, mine, the Meals on Wheels lady, presumably the ambulance men? And one set of unidentified prints in various parts of the house?"

My uncle nodded. "Fingerprints that are the same as those found in other houses that have been burgled, but nothing of any help to us, as we have no matches on our records."

"So someone unknown to the police?" I stated.

"Indeed. Someone unknown to us. But he's made a big mistake at this house. Until now it's only been burglary by deception. He's badly frightened these elderly ladies, but never physically hurt anyone – the opposite, in fact, pretending to be a polite and helpful meter reader who needed to use the loo, or welcomed a cup of tea – then rifled through handbags or drawers looking for money whilst his victim was distracted."

"This one went wrong, though," Laurie added. "Either Miss Catesby sussed him out or something else happened. Either way, as your uncle just said, our perpetrator has made a grave mistake by escalating burglary to cold-blooded murder." Under his breath he muttered, "Such a pity they abolished hanging in '69. I'd gladly put a noose round this bugger's neck myself."

I didn't say anything aloud, but I agreed with him.

I looked around the hall, trying to think what was the same, what was different. "It would have been most unusual for her to open the front door after dark. But open it, she obviously did?" I glanced at Laurie who nodded.

"Apart from where Meals on Wheels broke in, no sign of a forced entry."

"So he, or maybe she...?"

"More likely to be a 'he'," Uncle Toby advised.

"He, then. He came in and struck her with something. Before or after he'd looked round the place, I wonder? She fell... Was he leaving, not entering?" I was focussing now, thinking through scenarios, similar to how I think up scenes for the science fiction novel I was (attempting) to write. I pictured my characters doing things, saying things.

Laurie said, "The house has been, I won't say turned over, but definitely searched. He'd not have been able to do that with Miss Catesby conscious, so maybe he came in with his rehearsed spiel, didn't manage to send her off somewhere so he could be alone for a few minutes, lost his patience or temper and... *wham*." He mimed forcefully striking out. "Or, he attacked as soon as he stepped through the front door. Maybe forced his way in. She objected, he pushed her. Either way, she fell backwards... here." He pointed to the wall. "There are marks on the wallpaper along with hair and some blood, they match an injury to the back of her head. She was still conscious, though. She scrabbled, tried to get up by clinging to the telephone table – there are prints on the side of it – the puffin taxidermy got knocked off the table, shattered, and he hit her again, harder, knocking her out and breaking her jaw."

"He didn't hit her with the puffin did he?" That would be a last straw for me, for that creepy ornament.

"Doesn't look like it. The only thing that could have caused that sort of damage would have been the wooden base. It's been tested. Not a mark on it."

"Did he come with a weapon then, or use something else?" I looked around. The remains of the broken puffin. Two coats hanging on a coat rack, with a selection of umbrellas nestled in a huge blue china pot next to the half-moon glass telephone table that was attached to the wall.

"She liked umbrellas," I said. "She said they were far more elegant than a plastic mac." I touched one, royal blue with a silver shaft and a lovely, polished, wooden handle shaped like a horse's head. I'd always liked it. "She showed me this one once, it was her mother's. She said she never used it but kept it for sentimental value. I think this ring round it is silver. This one," I touched a black gentleman's umbrella that had a carved stag's antler for a handle, "this belonged to her fiancé, Albert. It had special meaning for her." I explained about Albert, then choking a little, moved on to the telephone table. "Could he have hit her with the telephone?" I suggested. "It's pretty heavy."

Laurie shook his head. "Nothing, only hers and the Meals on Wheels lady's fingerprints on the telephone."

"Where is her handbag?" I said, pointing to where she always had her bag next to the telephone.

"Forensics have it," Uncle Toby said. "We found the usual inside: handkerchief, door key, powder compact, lipstick, notebook and pencil. A packet of mints, a small diary and an address book – both with not many entries inside. We are trying to contact the people in the address book. No results so far."

"She didn't have any relatives," I said, biting my lip as another wave of grief tried to surface. "She was an only child, as were both her parents. They died twenty-five years ago, which is where she inherited the money to buy this house. Her fiancé was killed in the First World War. She'd been on her own all this time. Wasn't her purse in the bag?"

Uncle shook his head. "No purse."

"I know there *was* one in there, I saw it when she went to give me some money." I explained about the chocolate bar and Miss Catesby's generosity. Then described the purse, black, leather-looking plastic. I looked around; nothing caught my eye as being out of place, or wrong.

I went into the lounge, stepping around the chalk-marked outline. Drawers had been opened and searched through, cushions pulled off the sofa and the two fireside armchairs. I frowned, puzzled.

"Looking for money down the back of the seats," Laurie told me.

I shrugged, "I doubt he found anything." Then, noticing the armchairs again, a horrified thought struck me. "Where's Poppy, Miss Catesby's cat?"

Both my uncle and Laurie looked blank. "We've not seen a cat," they more-or-less answered together.

"She's black with white whiskers, white bib and tucker, little white mittens and a lop-sided white moustache. Surely, she must be here? Didn't anyone notice the tins of cat food, the cat basket and litter tray in the kitchen?"

"Yes, of course," Laurie answered. "But no cat."

No Poppy puss? I put her to one side of my mind, resolved to think about her being missing later. "This drawer in the sideboard, it should have..." I peered inside. "Should have had several books of Green Shield Stamps in here. You could ask her luncheon friend about them, though, for Miss Catesby did say, a few weeks before Christmas, that she was going to give them to her as a present." Green Shield stamps, coupon-like stamps given as incentives to buy things –

anything, including petrol – to collect and exchange for everyday items once enough of them filled a book. Some of the items in the GSS Catalogue were of luxury status, but it took years to collect enough stamps to redeem against these better items.

The kitchen and upstairs was the same mess, drawers pulled out and either searched through or contents tipped out onto the floor. Again, looking for money. In Miss Catesby's bedroom I gulped back another sob. There was the photograph of her sweetheart, Albert, beside her bed. The frame was broken, the photo ripped out. The bed itself had been stripped.

"A lot of old folks keep a note or two behind a picture, and money under the mattress," Laurie said.

"I honestly don't think Miss Catesby *had* any money to hide anywhere, she survived on her pension." I countered.

I felt a miserable failure as we walked back to the car. I hadn't been much help.

Correction. I had been *no* help at all. Something was nagging me, though. Something I knew I'd missed, but for the life of me I couldn't put my finger on what it was.

Then the thought of missing something vital vanished from my mind as I saw Poppy cowering under next door's car. I walked slowly over, bending slightly, my hand (the unbroken one) held out to her. "Poppy? Poppy puss? Come here girlie. It's me, Jan. You know me. Come on girl."

The poor little cat must have been terrified and hungry, shut outside all this time. She was soaked from the rain. To my huge relief she crawled out of hiding and came up to me, purring like a factory machine, rubbing her head round my ankles. I bent down and managed to scoop her up with one arm. I told Laurie to fetch a blanket from the car and to wrap it round me and her. "Soon get you dry, warm and fed, little girlie," I said, crooning to her. Then sent Laurie back inside the house to fetch some tins of cat food, the cat bed and litter tray from the kitchen.

"And where," Uncle Toby enquired, "do you intend to take her?"

I looked at him, eye to eye.

"Home of course. Basil will just have to learn to share."

I think my uncle was about to protest, but he knew me well enough not to attempt it.

18

DAY OF THE DALEKS

Poppy settled nicely at home. She spent the night curled at my feet on my bed, soon realised that her litter tray was in my bathroom, and ate as if she'd never been fed. Basil rarely came upstairs so the problem of them meeting and having pawsicuffs (the cat version of fisticuffs) would be confronted another day. For myself, my arm was hurting like heck. Monday morning would see me back at the hospital getting plastered. (For your sanity, I won't repeat the gin joke.)

I didn't see much of Uncle Toby or Laurie all day Saturday. Laurie arrived early, well before I woke up, and collected Uncle Toby and the Jag. It was times like this that being in a policeman's family had its drawbacks; Aunt Madge and I had barely seen either of them – apart from 'official business' for several days. Sitting by myself watching TV as the dusk turned the afternoon to a purplish-bruised sky outside, I again wondered if I really wanted to be a policeman's wife. A detective's wife, at that. Laurie had ambition, he was only recently promoted to the rank of Detective Sergeant, but he'd already said he wanted to make

Inspector one day. I was behind him all the way for that, he was a good cop. And believe me, *good* cops are rare. But did I want to have a future where all too often I rarely saw him? Where planned excursions or holidays were put on hold or even cancelled when some emergency hurtled in full, angry, force over the horizon? Where he came home at night tired and frustrated? Where I was left looking after the kids on my own... assuming we would eventually have children, that is.

I tried the telly, watched a couple of the races at Haydock on Grandstand, didn't care for the rugby or athletics, so tried reading, but it was difficult holding a book one-handed. Then a western came on: *Lancer: The Prodigal*. I turned the TV off; the series was poorly made and anyway, it was too much of a reminder of George Duffield and his brother. I pottered around a bit, dozed, made myself a cup of tea, then switched the TV on again at 5.45 ready for *Doctor Who*. Not that I was keen on Jon Pertwee as the Doctor, but this was to be the second episode of the series involving the Daleks – and who can resist a tin can on wheels with a blocked-drain plunger for an arm, trundling around and yelling in a tinny voice, *Exterminate*! *Exterminate*! Although it did occur to me as I settled down in the comfiest armchair, that I'd already had more than enough of 'extermination' these past few days.

The distinctive theme tune came on, which I sort of sung along to. *Tiddly-dum, tiddly-dum tiddly-tiddly-tiddly-dum. Whoo-hoo-hoo...* and the blasted doorbell rang. I cursed (a word which I doubt Uncle Toby, or even Laurie, knew I knew). I decided to ignore it. Aunt Madge was out with friends and wouldn't be home yet. But, anyway, she'd be putting her car into the garage at the side of the house, then come in through the back door into the kitchen. The doorbell rang again. I sighed, heaved myself to my feet and went to answer it.

I stood there, door wide open, blinking in surprise. A man stood there. I didn't immediately recognise him, not until he spoke.

He smiled. "Hello, love. I heard you'd been injured. Thought I'd pop by to see if you were all right. Did you find your ring?"

Joe. The bus conductor. What on earth was he doing here? I wasn't sure what to say, but came out with a rather feeble, "Yes, thank you, I did. How did you know I was injured?"

"Called in at your library, didn't I? Thought I'd get my old mum registered for this book delivery thing of yours. They told me you'd had an accident."

Did 'they' indeed!

"How do you know where I live?" I asked, suspiciously. I'd be pretty cross if my library colleagues had told him that as well.

He answered cheerily. "Seen you get off at the bus stop enough times. I knocked at one of the houses nearby and asked if they knew where the librarian lived. Nice lady with a whopping great big dog pointed this house out."

She had no right to do so, she could have been directing anybody here. Silly woman. Didn't she know that my uncle was a police officer – that my own father had been brutally gunned down by horrible men who had come knocking at our door? To be fair, it hadn't been *this* door, and no, she probably didn't know, but that wasn't the point. I then had another angry thought.

"Did you send me flowers and a rather unpleasant note?"

He frowned, shook his head. "Unpleasant note?

Why ever would I do that? I'm just trying to be friendly, you know."

"Someone anonymous sent it. I put the flowers in the bin and gave the note to my uncle. He is a Detective Chief Inspector." A slight lie about the flowers, but I thought giving my uncle's important rank might be useful.

Joe was still smiling, despite my increasing rude annoyance. "Nice house you have here, worth a bob or two, is it?"

"Yes, I expect it is, but if you'll excuse me, I'm supposed to be resting and I'm watching TV."

Still smiling, he nodded. "Yes, I can hear. That silly kiddies' *Doctor Who*. I thought you'd be interested in more sophisticated things. You won't invite me in for a cup of tea, then?"

"No, I won't!" I almost shouted it – the poor man probably meant well, but somehow he'd really got me spooked. I tried to calm myself, be more rational. "Look, I do appreciate your concern, but I really can't stand here talking. I'm on painkillers and they're making me woozy. Perhaps I'll see you next week. Goodbye."

With firm determination I shut the door and slid the safety chain on.

He stood there on the doorstep for a few minutes, then called out: "Suit yourself. I was only trying to be friendly." There was a thump. I don't know if he'd kicked or banged his fist on the door. Either way, I turned the hall light off so he couldn't see in through the small bubble-glass square window in the door, and then switched the outside lights on to illuminate the front garden.

Once again, I made sure all the doors were locked and pulled all the downstairs curtains closed. I then went upstairs to my aunt and uncle's front bedroom, not turning on the lights, and went to the window to look out. I couldn't see anyone outside. The garage was locked, so he wouldn't be able to get in through there, and the only place to hide would be if he squatted down behind Laurie's car, parked alongside the left-hand hedge. I watched for a bit. No moving shadows or anything. I began to relax. It looked like he'd gone. I made a mental note to use the bus at a different time in future.

After about ten minutes my thumping heart had steadied and I started to feel stupid. While there was no way that I would have asked him in, he *had* only intended to be friendly, poor chap, although I didn't fancy being here on my own for much longer. Should I call my uncle at the police station?

I sighed, pulled myself together. There was now no one outside and Uncle Toby would be home soon. I went back downstairs, but *Doctor Who* was just finishing. *It's Cliff Richard* was on next. He was all right, but not quite my thing, so I turned the TV off, put another two logs on the fire and sat and watched the comforting flames and fairy sparks as they danced up the chimney. I think I dozed off, for it seemed only minutes later that I heard the Jag pull up outside, but according to the clock on the mantlepiece, only about half an hour had passed. I got up to take the chain off the front door and let Uncle Toby and Laurie in. Both men looked absolutely exhausted.

"Dinner's in the slow cooker part of the Aga," I said to them as I hurried towards the kitchen, "It's chicken casserole, but you'll have to help me dish up, the pot's too heavy for one-handedness."

It didn't take the three of us long to eat our fill. Laurie offered to stay to help with the washing up, but Uncle Toby sent him off home. "Get yourself off, Sergeant. I'm going to put my feet up, catch the end of

Dixon of Dock Green, then see what the evening film is like. I doubt I'll be late to bed, it's been a tough week."

I didn't mention about my unwanted caller; the two important men in my life already had enough on their over-piled plates.

19

INTERLUDE - DS LAURIE WALKER

Jan's Aunt Madge was always generous with providing dinner for me. She maintained that it was as easy to cook for four as it was for three. I was grateful; back at my Section House digs it would have been baked beans on toast or soup. Funny how I was perfectly comfortable with calling Aunt Madge 'Aunt Madge' but her husband, my boss, remained 'sir'. I wonder if I'll still be calling him that at my wedding?

If a wedding takes place. Was it just me? Was I imagining things? Jan seemed to be remote, distant even. She wasn't wearing her engagement ring – OK I know she had to take it off her finger because of the broken arm, but could she not have slid it onto her right hand? And where was it anyway? I hadn't said anything when she'd confessed that she'd left it at the old lady's house, having to bite my tongue though. How could she have been so careless? That ring cost a lot of money – more than an entire month's wages.

And tonight? She didn't seem too pleased to see me. No kiss on the cheek when I'd walked in with her uncle, and dinner was consumed almost in silence. I looked at her a couple of times across the dining room table, but she kept her gaze cast downward, pretending to concentrate on eating one-handed. But I knew there was something wrong.

Wrong with me perhaps? Had she changed her mind?

It had been a long day, a long week. Two murders that we were nowhere near moving forward with. Beyond the little we had already established nothing new had come to light for either of them, apart from we'd managed to find a relative, of sorts, for Miss Catesby. The sensible old girl had made a will, a copy of which we found in a bureau drawer. In it, she named an Arthur James Wilfred Barrowstone, brother to her deceased fiancé as her heir – or, '*should he be deceased, to be shared between any surviving offspring*'. Someone, as a beneficiary, was going to be delighted.

Fortunately, it was not a common surname, as a search through a telephone directory for something like Smith or Jones would have been impossible, but we hit the target square on at the third telephone call. Arthur Barrowstone had passed away back in 1962 but his son, Julian, was, ironically, living a few miles away in Loughton, the other side of Epping Forest. He had only vaguely known about an uncle who had been killed in the Great War, but had no idea about Miss Catesby. It would take several legal checks by the probate lawyers to establish, beyond doubt, that this Julian Barrowstone was the only, legitimate, heir but from the documents he showed us we were pretty certain that we had the right guy. Especially when we compared Miss Catesby's photographs with a few he had – there was no mistaking that Albert and Arthur were brothers, as they were almost two peas in a pod. And then he showed us an exact copy of Miss Catesby's group photograph taken on the day she'd become engaged to Albert Barrowstone. The day before the two men had gone off to war. Such a shame that a lonely old lady had not known about the man who would have been her nephew by marriage.

It did occur to us that here, with this will, was a motive for murder, but Mr Barrowstone's surprise at learning about Miss Catesby seemed genuine.

"I knew my father lost an older brother in the Great War," he'd said when he came into the police station, "and that he'd had a sweetheart, but beyond the photograph, knew nothing about her. My father never mentioned his brother, nor either of the wars for that matter, so we did not even know the lady's name." I totally believed him, as did DCI Christopher.

You get a nose for the truth or lies. Mr Barrowstone was telling the truth.

I hated not being able to get any further with this case. Hated not being able to look through the fog when someone's life had been brutally taken through an act of hatred, revenge, spur of the moment anger. Whatever triggered it, murder was murder. A life had been deliberately taken, usually leaving other lives in its wake shattered to pieces. Grieving husbands, wives, parents, brothers, sisters. Fatherless, motherless children, distraught parents. On both sides of the coin, for the family of the perpetrator and the victim.

What made these cases so, oh I don't know, so *dispassionate*, was the apparent lack of care. No one *cared* that two people were dead. There was no one, apart from a distant relative and a twin brother who couldn't stand his dead brother anyway.

Maybe I was tired. I needed a good night's sleep, I'd hardly had one since we'd got back from Devon. That was a good time, a good holiday – despite the interruption of finding human remains in my dad's compost heap.

There was lemon tart and cream for pudding. DCI

Christopher helped Jan serve it. Was that a flicker of a smile on her face as she placed the dish in front of me? I couldn't be certain.

I realised I ought to say something. What? "Was *Doctor Who* good tonight?" A neutral question, I thought. Jan shrugged, admitted that she hadn't watched it.

"I fell asleep in front of the fire," she said. I'm a policeman. I knew she was lying.

She did kiss me at the front door, a peck on the cheek. I took the bull by the horns.

"Is everything OK?" I asked, dreading a negative answer.

She smiled. Jan has the loveliest smile.

"I'm tired and my arm is really hurting. I think I'll leave Uncle Toby to the telly and go to bed."

"Has the cat settled?" Now why didn't I think of asking her that earlier?

Her smile brightened. "Yes, she's been curled on my bed all day. I'll expect a nice warm spot beneath the covers for my feet."

"I don't know if we've got to go into the Station or not tomorrow, but if not, do you fancy going for a drive or something? Lunch somewhere, a nice pub perhaps? Or I might have to drive to the Isle of Wight next week. Hampshire police have drawn a blank with finding our fisherman."

To my disappointment Jan shook her head. "It's sweet of you, but jolting around in a car is going to hurt even more. Once I get a cast on maybe things will feel better?"

I nodded agreement, gave her a quick kiss and, collecting my overcoat from the coat rack, went out the front door. It had started raining again, but I didn't bother putting my coat on, it was a few steps to the car, although I was honestly fed up to the back teeth with rain and getting wet.

"Shut the door and get back into the warm," I called. Jan blew me a kiss and did so, closing the door and shutting me out in the wet night.

My car was parked at the side by the hedge. I had to fumble for my keys, found them, fumbled some more in the shadows to open the driver's side door. I leant in to toss my coat onto the passenger seat, felt, rather than heard movement behind me... I was half in the car, half out. I backed out, partially turning, expecting to see Jan or DCI Christopher behind me.

Something hit me, hard, on the back of the head. I fell forward across the driver's seat. Knew nothing more.

20

BATS AND FROGS

I stayed up with Uncle Toby after all, partly because I was too weary to go upstairs. He'd kindly taken up a dish of cat food for Poppy when he went to change into something more comfortable than his suit, then we both started on the film. It wasn't very good. A pilot for a possible series, with American actors that neither of us knew. This chap ran San Francisco Airport his way, much to the chagrin of his boss. The plot was a boy's parents were divorcing and so he stole a small plane, (I mean a young boy knew how to fly a plane? Aw, c'mon!) and thieves tried to steal a money shipment. Terribly far fetched, poorly scripted and extremely boring. Both Uncle Toby and I fell asleep, which says it all, doesn't it?

We woke to Aunt Madge coming in at around nine-thirty.

"It's raining bats and frogs out there!" she exclaimed shaking water everywhere as she took off her coat.

'Bats and frogs' had been invented by us one November when I was little, instead of the more familiar saying 'cats and dogs'. More than that basic explanation I absolutely cannot remember. I assume we were at a firework night party and it was raining. Rain? How extraordinary! (She said, sarcastically.) However it came about, 'bats and frogs' on a rainy day it has been ever since.

"Where's Laurie?" Aunt Madge asked as she hurried to the fire in order to poke it back into life. (Uncle and I had been remiss, and had let it die down while we slept.)

"He went back to his digs soon after we'd eaten," I said yawning and stretching – then 'ouching' and wincing, having irritated my be-slinged arm.

Aunt Madge frowned at us, puzzled. "So what's wrong with his car then? It's still outside."

I looked at Uncle Toby. He looked at me. We both looked, baffled, at Aunt Madge as if she'd suddenly burst into Double Dutch gibberish.

Shaking his head, frowning, Uncle Toby went to the window, peered behind the curtain. "Wait here," he said gruffly as he headed for the front door.

Madge and I followed, watched him from the door. He leant into Laurie's car, bobbed up again shouted at us.

"Call an ambulance, get blankets! *Hurry*!"

I was shaking as the ambulance drove away with my Laurie and Uncle Toby inside. I was in the car with Aunt Madge, following behind.

Laurie had come round a little before the ambulance men arrived, but he was confused and dizzy, in a bad way. His legs and feet were soaked through, but at least his top half, where he'd been slumped inside the car, was dry. He was frozen through – it was January – and blood from a vicious cut to the back of his head had trickled down his cheek. Between them, my aunt and uncle half-walked, half-carried him indoors, sat him in front of the fire. As well as I could I pulled off his sodden shoes and socks and wrapped his feet in a couple of my warm, fluffy jumpers that Aunt Madge had grabbed from my bedroom.

His teeth were chattering as he tried to talk, but we all told him to shut up. Uncle Toby had been filling a couple of hot water bottles, which we placed against Laurie's chest and back – Aunt Madge was a first-aider, she told us not to rub or try to over-warm the extremities as that would cause cold blood to flow back to the essential organs. We wrapped warm blankets round him, one over his head so only his pale face showed. Thank goodness the ambulance had arrived quickly!

All the way to the hospital I was crying, devastated that I hadn't realised he'd not driven off. What had been the matter with me? I always, *always* either stood at the front door or the window to wave goodbye. Always, always, *always*... but not tonight. Not tonight when it had really mattered.

Uncle Toby was anxious to find out what had happened, but Laurie was in no fit state to talk, and as soon as we reached Whipps Cross Casualty, Laurie was whisked off to X-ray and lord knows where else. The three of us sat in the uncomfortable-chaired waiting area, and waited. Aunt Madge had thought to make a flask of coffee while the ambulance men had been checking Laurie over – she was so unflappable and efficient. I took a couple of sips from the plastic flask cup then handed it to Uncle Toby, and suddenly poured out in a torrent of words, intermixed with sobs, everything that had happened. Words which were interspersed every so often with, "I should have told you earlier," and "*Why* didn't I tell you earlier?"

"No good whying and whereforing, Jan, that'll get us nowhere. You say this was the bus conductor who called?"

"Yes, Joe something. He's always seemed so nice. I felt mean after I'd shut the door in his face because I realised that he'd only come round to be kind."

"Seems like he might not have been so kind after all," Uncle Toby said, "but we could be jumping to the wrong conclusion. Maybe it wasn't him who attacked my sergeant?"

"If it wasn't him, there's rather a big coincidence, though, isn't there?" Aunt Madge observed.

It was not far off midnight before the doctor came to see us, and as he was all smiles we relaxed.

"DS Walker is fine," he assured us. "He'll have one heck of a headache for a while, mind you, as that was some thump he received – ten stitches, a lump the size of a duck egg and a bald patch where we had to shave the hair away, but no skull fracture and no lasting damage. We've taken him up to a ward for tonight, keep him under observation, just in case, but I suggest you all go home and get some sleep. Come and get him tomorrow, elevenish, I'd say, after Rounds."

"Can I see him now?" I almost whispered it, I was so anxious.

"No, miss, he'll be tucked up in bed, and there's no visiting this time of night. Go home and get some sleep."

We did as he suggested, although I didn't sleep well, tossing and turning and swapping between the anxiety in my heart and head, and the shooting pain in my arm.

21

PHOTOGRAPHS

I pleaded with Aunt Madge to go with her to collect Laurie the next morning, but she flatly refused. For one thing it took me ages (with Aunt Madge's gentle help) to get washed, dressed and my sling re-slung, plus she said that getting in and out of the car wasn't easy for me. "You'll be better off putting the kettle on for when we get back, and ensuring there are clean towels and such in the spare room."

We'd already agreed that Laurie was to come home to us and stay for as long as it took – even if he did protest, as he probably would. Two patients. Our own little cottage hospital.

I managed to make Uncle Toby a coffee at around ten-thirty and carried it into him in his den – a small back room where he kept all his papers and policeman stuff. During the day, when he was at work, the door was kept locked, not because he didn't trust us, but we had a cleaner, Mrs P, who came in twice a week, and Aunt Madge often had friends round for morning coffee or afternoon tea, so it was safer to ensure his room was kept out of bounds.

Unfortunately, given that it was Sunday there was

nothing he could do about tracking Joe down. Buses still ran, but as a depleted Sunday Service, and all administration offices were closed. Uncle Toby had sent two constables from his team to uncover some information, but they had drawn a blank. Drivers, conductors, mechanics and an inspector were at the local depot but no clerical staff, and no one seemed to know where Joe lived. All he had established was that a conductor named Joe Briggs, who worked the 69 route, had called in sick. Annoyingly frustrating, but any further investigation would have to wait until first thing Monday morning, and while a deliberate attack on a police officer was important, finding the murderer of an old lady was even more essential before he struck – literally – again.

My uncle had black and white photographs laid out over the table, which served as a desk. I didn't intentionally look, but couldn't help seeing. Miss Catesby. Photos taken at her house as she lay dead on the floor.

"Poor woman," I muttered, "she didn't deserve any of this."

"No one does, Cupcake."

"Can I look at these properly?" I said, hesitantly.

"If you want to, but are you sure?"

I shook my head. "Absolutely not, but maybe I'll spot something you've missed, and there's still something bothering me. Something *I've* missed."

He handed me one of the photos, a close up of Miss Catesby's head where the ooze of blood had dried round the bruising to her face. I swallowed hard, took a couple of breaths to steady myself and studied the image.

"I didn't think bruises formed after death?" was the first thing I said.

"They don't. Sadly it seems she was alive but

unconscious for several hours. She died of the cold and a heart attack."

"So will that still be murder?" I asked.

"A good lawyer might argue for aggravated assault, or manslaughter. It depends on whether the violence was intentional. Premeditated, or an accident."

"So if you find and arrest the person who did this, and prove the injury was not accidental...?"

"Then it will be murder, yes."

I looked carefully at the half-moon shape of the heavy bruise on her face and the broken skin where something heavy had caught her. "It's rather a distinct shape, isn't it? There seems to be a sort of ridged pattern, or am I imagining things?" I observed.

I got a familiar, uncommitted, "*Mmm hmm*," as a reply.

"Horseshoe shaped. Like that wonderful bruise Aunt Madge had on her thigh after she'd been kicked that time." I hasten to add, not by one of *our* horses, but by a mare which had been frightened and lashed out unexpectedly.

Uncle Toby selected a different photograph and looked at it. Nodded. "You're right, but this wasn't done by a horse, alas."

"But maybe a horse's *shoe*?"

Uncle Toby smiled and took a sip of the coffee I'd brought him. "Quite possibly, except, yet again, where would the horse fit in? I don't think the dear old lady was anywhere near a stable yard."

"No, of course not, but there is a horseshoe on the small windowsill next to the front door. I painted it silver, stuck some artificial flowers on it and gave it to her for her birthday last year. We'd been talking about good and bad luck, you see, and she said she could do with something lucky, so I obliged." I paused, reflectively. Added gloomily, "It didn't bring her much luck did it?"

"Apparently not. A horseshoe, you say?" Uncle Toby looked closely at a couple more of the photographs, then, rising from his chair he gathered the photos up. "You be all right on your own for a while?"

I hardly had time to answer for he was out the front door and backing the Jag out of the garage.

"Was it something I said?" I remarked to the empty house.

22

DEAD END

Sunday, so far, was turning out to be not as anyone had planned. Aunt Madge returned from the hospital at around midday, empty-handed. Laurie was fine, she assured me, slipping off her high heels and stepping into her fluffy slippers. (New. A Christmas present.)

"The consultant is slightly concerned about lingering concussion, and given Laurie's job, wants to ensure that he is 100% before being discharged."

I was devastated. "I should have gone with you!" I wailed.

"You can go this afternoon at visiting time. Where's Toby?"

"No idea. I assume at work." I told her about my theory of the horseshoe.

She tutted. "Will he be back for Sunday lunch, then? Not that we'll be having a roast, I haven't even started doing it yet."

More gloom for me. I should have started dinner. And another reminder that being the wife of a policeman was not always plain sailing. "I'm sorry, I couldn't peel the potatoes. And I didn't know what else you might want me to do."

Aunt Madge gave me a quick kiss of reassurance. "At this precise moment, my dear, all I want is a nice cup of tea and a chocolate biscuit or two. Shall I do the roast for dinner this evening instead of lunchtime?"

Just as well the roast beef and Yorkshire pud had not been scheduled for the usual one o'clock, as Uncle Toby didn't get back until nearly 2 p.m. as Aunt Madge and I were about to leave for the hospital again.

"The horseshoe was a dead end I'm afraid Jan," he said solemnly as he put the kettle on to make himself coffee. "It was there, on the windowsill as you said, but didn't look like it had been moved for months. A layer of dust round it, and from what I could tell, nothing incriminating on it except for a cobweb and a dead spider."

I was crestfallen. I was sure that I had cracked a good clue. So we were back to the drawing board, none the wiser for anything.

"Never mind, it was a good thought," Laurie said as I sat on a hard chair next to his hospital bed. He was receiving special care as they had transferred him to a quiet, private, side ward. He said it was because of him being a Detective Sergeant; I said it was because he looked like Cary Grant and all the nurses secretly fancied him.

"Probably a few doctors too," he laughed.

I didn't understand the joke. I knew I was missing something when he made these sort of references, but I didn't know exactly *what* I was missing. I'll be the first to admit that I was a rather naïve almost-nineteen-year-old and many an innuendo passed me by. Either the penny would drop for me at some point, or I ought to consider reading some different books or

I would need to summon the courage to ask Aunt Madge.

I'd told Laurie my theory, and filled him in with everything he'd missed – my unwanted apparent admirer, and my idea about the horseshoe.

"You're right about that bruise to Miss Catesby's face being a curved shape, but it might just have been the way he struck her. Forensics will have more of an insight. I assume your uncle will be updating them?"

"Yes, it's on his 'to do' list for tomorrow, alongside arresting that wretched bus conductor." I'd stopped calling him 'Joe'. Using his name seemed too familiar and friendly. I now hated him.

"It might not have been him who attacked me, you know Jan." He blushed a bit. "You're a lovely girl, and I can understand other men liking you."

I snorted. Of course it was him. And I didn't want men like that liking me.

We talked of a few other things, but nothing to do with weddings or engagement party plans. I did wonder, at the back of my mind, whether Laurie was changing his mind. I would have to raise the elephant in the room subject at some point, I guessed, but perhaps a hospital side ward was not the appropriate time or place.

"By the way," he said, "did we tell you that the post-mortem report had come back for Gerald Duffield?"

I half-smiled. Gory post-mortem reports *were* a more appropriate conversation for a hospital ward. "Go on, tell me the worst," I said. "I'll not throw up."

"It seems there was nothing wrong with your chap's heart. In fact, Jack Carlton, the pathologist, said that Duffield was an extremely fit and healthy man for his age."

"No!" I gasped. "The lying old bug! You mean to

say he was perfectly able to get around? Up and down stairs or get to the library himself?"

Laurie nodded, "Seems so. He would have been perfectly fit enough to have been called up. Seems he faked his exemption papers."

"Ooh, if he wasn't already dead, I'd kill him myself!" I exclaimed, then blushed bright red. That was a terrible thing to say!

"The information might give us another idea for a motive. We're at a dead end so far."

I hated to say it, but, "Maybe George finally found out. Or Mr Norton, next door?"

"All part of our ongoing enquiries," was all Laurie replied.

We talked a bit more about nothing in particular – still not mentioning any wedding plans – and by four o'clock Laurie was looking tired. He was desperately trying to hide it, but his head kept drooping and he'd jerk upright again and wince. If he was on the same or similar painkillers to me, then I wasn't in the least surprised. They had enough kick to knock out one of Aunt Madge's horses.

"I think I'd better go," I said, standing up and rubbing my numb backside. "You're almost asleep – and it's sleep you need, that's why you're in this quiet room."

Did he look disappointed, or relieved?

"You sorted to get home?" he asked, concerned.

"Yes, I'll get a taxi. No problem." Ordinarily, without my arm in a sling and hurting abysmally I would have caught a bus. But I wasn't too keen on buses at this precise moment. And anyway, Uncle Toby had given me the money for the taxi fare.

"Oh, I brought you this to borrow," I said, as I stood up and handed him a paper bag that had been on the floor by my feet. "I thought he would keep you company, but you don't have to have him if you think it's silly."

Laurie opened the bag and brought out my teddy bear.

"It's Bee Bear!" he laughed. "Hello mate. I bet the nurses will start cooing over you far more than they do me."

"If you think having him with you is a bit childish..." I began.

"Nonsense. He's wonderful. I can tell him all my woes and grumbles and he'll not say a word back, or ever repeat them."

"He might do," I laughed. "I've planted a listening device in his tummy."

Laurie chuckled, held up my teddy, rattled him, then inspected the stitching of all his seams. "Don't take this wrong, Jan love, but I know the standard of your sewing. These neat little stitches ain't of your doin' darlin'."

I kissed Laurie – and Bee Bear – goodbye, and managed to keep a straight face as I opened the door.

"Well, Mr Smarty Pants," I said, grinning, "I bribed Aunt Madge to do the sewing."

Hah! That would keep him thinking.

23

PLASTERED

In a way it was convenient that I had my appointment with the plaster casterers on the Monday morning, as we'd received a telephone call at about 9.30 from Laurie giving the glad news that he could be discharged as soon as someone could collect him. Two birds with one stone, as it were.

Uncle Toby said he'd 'do the honours' as Aunt Madge had her own appointment that same morning (annual booster vaccinations for the horses – one of the stable girls could have seen to it, but my aunt preferred to be there herself). So it was that after another X-ray, and while Uncle Toby went off in search of Laurie to bail him out, I was sitting in the 'broken bones' department waiting my turn to have a cast plastered around my arm. (Why do hospitals have such uncomfortable chairs for people who are already uncomfortable enough?)

A woman – young lady? Girl? – hobbled in with her crutches and a plaster cast on her leg and sat down opposite me. I think we stared at one another for half-a-minute or so, then she said, grinning, "It *is* Jan isn't it?"

I laughed because I'd almost spoken at the same moment: "It *is* Janet isn't it?"

For a few years we'd been at school together in the same class, Wellington Avenue Secondary School for Girls. We'd come to an agreement where we did each other's homework for the couple of subjects we were hopeless at; an agreement which was short-lived as we soon got caught out and had to do detention and lines. I never told my aunt and uncle, though – of the cheating or the detention.

Janet's parents moved before we went up to the GCE exam year at fifteen. She didn't move far away, but it was far enough for two teenagers who were not independently mobile to drift apart. I'd missed her as I didn't have other friends. Nearly all the girls in our year said I was weird because I was always reading books or writing stories. I thought that was normal, (didn't everyone read or write for pleasure?) until one spiteful girl told me to my face, while poking me in the chest with her finger that I was 'warped in the head', although she'd added several unrepeatable, defamatory and unkind words to that small bit; words referring to me not having a father and being a spoilt, rich kid. (The word she used was not 'kid', my father had been murdered, I was not spoilt and while we were comfortably off, we weren't rich.) I was thirteen and it upset me deeply. Apart from Janet, I'd kept myself to myself at school after that.

Sitting in the hospital waiting room, we exchanged sympathetic notes on how we'd come about our injuries: she'd broken her ankle ice-skating, and was here to have the cast removed. I explained I was here to have one put on.

"Where are you working?" I asked her. She told me she was doing secretarial work in London for a big law firm, and I told her about the library.

"Your uncle still a policeman?" she asked. "A lot of the girls were scared of you because of that. They thought he'd arrest them for being so horrid to you if you ever snitched."

I grimaced at that. "I wish I'd known, I would have used it to more advantage. But no, I never mentioned the bullying. I hid myself away behind my long hair and buried myself deeper in my books."

Janet shook her head, her lips pressed close together. "The more horrid ones called you 'Booknosey', did you know that? Some of them were such cows."

No I didn't know. Perhaps it was just as well; they'd hurt me enough at school with their name-calling as it was, especially after Janet had left and I had to fend for myself.

She told me that she'd recently become engaged and showed me her engagement ring, and I said, "Me too," but couldn't show her my ring as I didn't have it. I did suddenly wonder if Aunt Madge still had it in her handbag. I felt awful as I'd completely forgotten about it, (again!)

"Do you remember those hats and the policeman?" she asked, laughing.

"Oh gosh! Yes!" I laughed too. "We were on our way to the Friday night dance at the Wellington Avenue Youth Club, and we had those Robin Hood hats on. We thought we were the bee's knees."

"Yes, and a young copper on the other side of the road called out, 'Rotten hats!'."

"And you, you terror," I finished the story, "shouted back, 'They're better than yours!' I nearly died of embarrassment."

We were laughing so much the nurse had to call my name twice.

By the time I re-emerged with my arm encased in

plaster and tucked inside a sling for comfort, Janet had gone, but sitting in her place was Laurie, looking pale but alive and otherwise healthy. I flung my good arm around his neck and hugged him tight.

"Your uncle's waiting for us in the car. He said he'll drop you off home, then get to the Station. Hopefully, they'd have brought your bus conductor in for questioning by the time we get there."

"We?" I queried.

"Yes. I'm fine, I'd like to get back to work."

I didn't agree with that, but there was no point in arguing with him.

We walked, arm in arm (my good arm, that is) to the car park where Uncle Toby was waiting reading through a file for something or other.

"I don't really want to be at home on my own." I said, nervously, as we got into the car. "At least, not until I'm sure you have 'him' safe in custody. Am I being silly?"

Uncle, who was driving, looked at me in the rear-view mirror. "Sounds reasonable to me. How about we have a spot of lunch in the police canteen?"

Laurie laughed. "Is that the best we can offer, sir?"

Uncle countered indignantly, "Flo is always welcoming, and you can't say that her sausage and mustard sandwiches aren't delicious."

"That I can't," Laurie answered with a grin, "but the sausages *are* more fat than sausage."

"I prefer chunky sausages," Uncle Toby replied.

"Ah, but there's chunky and there's fatty."

I put an end to the good-natured quibbling by saying: "It probably isn't up to Flo regarding which cheap brand of sausages she has to buy."

The canteen was upstairs at the back of the police station, a small room with a serving hatch to one side, but had rather uninspiring décor with its yellowy cream walls and brown lino on the floor. It was spotlessly clean, though. Flo, the canteen supervisor, and her few staff members made up for the impression of gloom by being lovely, cheerful people – and (apart from the greasy sausages) good cooks if anyone wanted a hot meal. Flo regarded her customers as one big family – from the newest rookie to the Chief Constable, and made sure that her coffee tasted like coffee and her tea was good, strong tea. As it turned out Uncle Toby was right about the sandwiches and Laurie was right about the sausages. While absolutely scrummy, they were a tad fatty.

While we ate, I studied some of the pictures on the walls. Flo insisted on nice paintings (reproduction, of course) not police crime posters. "My canteen" she would say to visitors or policemen alike, "is for R and R, not work." She had two countryside watercolours painted by Aunt Madge, *Sunflowers* by van Gogh, a Turner, a Constable and a Renoir.

I was staring at the Renoir. The Umbrellas. I was always fascinated by it whenever I was in the canteen, or rather it was the red-haired woman carrying a basket that I liked. She had such lovely eyes and I always found myself wondering who she was and what she was thinking. The more I looked, the quieter I became.

Laurie noticed my silence. "You all right, love?"

I shook my head, bit my lip. "That painting. I've just realised what it is that's been bugging me all this time."

24

INTERLUDE - DS LAURIE WALKER

"It's the umbrellas." Jan had said in the canteen, her cup of tea going cold in her hand. "There was Albert's umbrella, the lovely blue one belonging to Miss Catesby's mother, and two more ladies' umbrellas, a red one and a green one. But I've just realised, there was another one. Another gentleman's umbrella. It shouldn't be there." She'd gulped back tears and said in a horrified whisper, "It should be in London Transport's lost property department."

Everything swung into action after that. We stuffed down the last of the sandwiches, DCI Christopher arranged for someone to take Jan home, and a warrant was hastily put out for Joseph Briggs' arrest. We found him, some hours later, at the pub he usually frequented, hiding in the gents' lav. His mother, elderly but by no means disabled or bedridden, as he'd claimed, had openly told us where he might be. I have to say, she was a less than caring mother. Her exact words to me were, "So what has the little creep been up to this time?" Well, not *exact* words. She used something much more vulgar than 'creep'.

DCI Christopher had personally retrieved the

additional gent's umbrella from Miss Catesby's house and shouted at a few people to get it to forensics for an immediate analysis. For once, 'immediate' only meant three hours, for the conclusive report came back that the solid, curved wooden handle had traces of blood and hair on it, and confirmed that the item had the initials H.L.J. engraved on a silver ring below the handle. Without a shadow of doubt, this was the weapon used, and the umbrella that belonged to Jan's driver. Harry. The one she had left on the bus.

"Anyone could've picked it up," Briggs protested when we confronted him in the interview room with the damning evidence.

"Not everyone could have lain in wait to assault my sergeant, or pester my niece." The DCI had countered in his quiet voice, that to those of us who knew him, signified immense anger.

"I didn't pester her. I was concerned for her. I like her."

Unfortunately, Briggs then muttered, "She doesn't deserve you. I should've hit you harder." Which both DCI Christopher and I heard. The guy had condemned himself. Later, confirmation came through for corresponding fingerprints. Those on the umbrella were his and were an exact match for the collection of prints we had from other burgled houses. We'd got him!

It seemed that Briggs augmented his pay by pretending to be a gas meter reader – his bus conductor's uniform doubling for something that resembled the uniform worn by Gas Board men. He would only steal cash, or Green Shield stamps if he came across them, and had made a pretty penny these last few months. Most of which, from what we later established, he spent at the pub on beer and spirits or betting on the horses. Bets that he invariably lost. He was in debt by several thousand pounds.

He confessed everything once he realised he'd put his size 10s in his mouth, and admitted to the gambling addiction. He'd started by following an elderly woman home after he'd finished his shift several months back. Had boldly knocked at her door, said he was the gas man, walked in, went down her bag and came away with over fifty pounds in his pocket. Spurred on by success after success he'd gradually become bolder, hanging around by the cemetery gates in addition to following women home from the bus terminus. "I chose them who were flustered or upset after visiting a grave, or had a heavy shopping bag, which usually meant they was on their way home. Easy peasy targets."

He laughed, actually laughed as he said that. For our part we now had another witness to identify him. Jan's library lady, Mrs Chelmsford, had apparently seen him loitering by the cemetery gates. Poor Jan, she'd been so upset when she finally remembered to tell us that bit of the puzzle. Not her fault; if it hadn't been for the umbrella, nothing would have made sense anyway.

"The silly old biddies always put their handbags down on a table in the hall as soon as they get home. I give them a minute, then knock at the door. Most of them still have their coats on and are in a tizz. It's like taking candy from a baby."

"And Miss Catesby?" DCI Christopher asked. His voice was low, I knew he was furious.

"Who?" Briggs said. Cheeky sod.

"The woman you hit round the head. The woman who you left on the floor to die."

Briggs snorted. "Don't know anyone like that. I never killed no one, just went down their bags and drawers." He sniggered. "Cupboard drawers, not their knickers."

I could quite cheerfully have landed him one.

"Why did you hit her?" my guvnor asked.

Briggs shrugged, stuffed his hands in his jeans' pockets. I guessed he'd not be wearing jeans again for a long while, he'd soon be in prison overalls.

He shrugged again, and wiped his hand under a running nose. Admitted, "Silly old bat kept wittering on and on and wouldn't let me in. That stuck up niece of yours had let on where an old girl lived – she'd left her ring there. I wondered whether to lift it if it were still there, couldn't find it. It had been raining a lot an' when the bus got to the terminus, I noticed an umbrella in the luggage hole. Didn't know it were your spoilt little madam's. I liked her, you know. Idiot that I am. Of course the posh little miss wouldn't be interested in a common bus conductor. I should've known better. Had no idea who'd left that umbrella, so I took it an' decided to see if I could find the old girl's house. Bloody inspector kept me talking, insisted I had this that 'n the other paperwork to do before I could get off. I had a quick cuppa an' a bite to eat at the café over the road, then headed for the old girl's place. I nearly ducked out when I saw all them police cars in Leawood, but I figured they was busy elsewhere, so it gave me a clear run."

"So, stealing from Miss Catesby wasn't the doddle you expected it to be? She would not co-operate. You got angry and hit her."

"It were an accident. I needed the money to pay off a debt on a horse. A certainty it was supposed to 'ave been. Huh, ruddy thing didn't get over the first ruddy jump, did it? The umbrella was in me hand and I bashed the handle against the old girl's head. I only meant t' knock her aside. She weren't dead when

I left her, so it ain't my ruddy fault she pegged it, is it?"

"You left her, injured, on the floor while you searched her house. Then left her there. Left her with a fractured jaw and a split skull." I too was talking low, as furious as my boss.

"Left her to die. As you would have left my Detective Sergeant had he not been found," DCI Christopher said.

Briggs just glared at me with eyes filled with jealousy. Refused to say anything else.

Did he really think that my darling Jan would fancy him? She has more sense than that, for all that she isn't all that 'worldy-wise', but that's one of the endearing things about her. Why I love her so much. She's an innocent.

I recited Briggs' rights, and arrested him for assaulting a policeman, multiple burglaries – and murder.

A pity we didn't have the same breakthrough for the first homicide. Two victims, as it had turned out, on the same night and within a few minutes' walk of each other. But for Gerald Duffield's murder we'd drawn a total blank.

25

ASHES TO ASHES

Two funerals in two days. I felt that I had to go to both, even though I had never particularly liked Gerald Duffield. Uncle Toby and Aunt Madge had brought me up to respect the truth, loyalty, personal honour and duty. This might sound like old-fashioned ideals, but they were solid, important ideals.

My uncle, quietly, and not that often, privately expressed his concern about the corruption and outright dishonesty that permeated the police force. He said that bad behaviour had been rife ever since the days of the original Bow Street Runners and then the early Peelers and Bobbies. Officers, from constables to chief superintendents were all too capable of turning blind eyes and sweeping things under carpets, especially if easy shortcuts for arrests were needed, regardless of the truth or whether the wrong person was charged, tried and sent to prison. Too many were all too quick to accept bribes and backhanders, were biased against people with a different coloured skin, religion or race, and sexist against women. In too many forces, assaults on fellow policemen who did not conform to the corruption, were common. To possible civilian suspects, harassment, violence and sexual offences were meted out on a daily basis in too many places. Uncle Toby – and Laurie – would have none of any of it. If the lawmakers did not respect the law what hope was there for keeping the law? Some officers from other areas disliked my uncle for his moral stance. Fortunately, as many admired him.

I went to Gerald Duffield's funeral out of a deep-rooted sense of respect. And also to see who else was there in case anything joggled some additional memory, a clue which could give a motive for his death, and perhaps point to a suspect. So far, that side of this murder enquiry was a complete blank.

All four of us attended the cremation service, Uncle Toby and Laurie as this was their case, and Aunt Madge to give me moral support.

There were quite a few people attending, relatives from the brothers' father's side, and masters from the school where Gerald taught, with a few now grown-up former pupils, although I rather suspected that they were there to ensure they were finally rid of him. George was there, naturally, with the cousin who had been looking after him, her family accompanying her. It seemed that her son was looking for accommodation in the Chingford area, having recently started a new job at Walthamstow Town Hall in the planning department, so he was to take Gerald's upstairs flat for a lower than usual rent, and to keep an eye on George as part of the bargain. He seemed a pleasant enough young man. He even thanked me for bringing books to George, and previously to Gerald. Which was nice of him, though I suspect it was only motivated by politeness. It did, cynically, cross my mind that getting a cheap flat could be a motive for murder, but I decided that such an uncharitable thought was scraping the bottom of a barrel and pushing conjecture a bit too far.

To my utter surprise, Mr Norton was there as well, with a friend pushing him in a wheelchair. Given the animosity expressed by both parties I'm afraid I couldn't help wondering if there was an ulterior motive: a need to publicly prove innocence?

"Is Paul Norton still a suspect?" I whispered to Laurie. "I don't like him much and he didn't like Gerald or George."

He shook his head, whispered back, "No. And like or dislike is no reason to suspect someone. Norton gives the impression of being hale and hearty, but he's riddled with arthritis. That's why he had to retire from his job."

"Which was?"

Laurie seemed surprised that I didn't know. "He was a journalist for one of the big papers. Couldn't type anymore, so he was 'let go' as they crudely say. Haven't you ever noticed how slowly he walks and how gnarled his hands? I doubt he would have had the strength to hold that screwdriver to use it." Laurie squeezed my hand. "You might have misjudged him, you know. He was one of the leading book review critics."

I felt cross, embarrassed and ashamed. Why hadn't he told me about his job? So he had every right to be critical. (Although I still thought he was wrong about Anne McAffrey's book!) Of course I'd noticed his hands, and I'd known, deep down, that he was disabled enough to be genuinely on my B.D.S. route, but I had never really looked beyond his grumpiness. Or taken real notice of him.

I mentioned my guilt to Aunt Madge that afternoon, back home. The cousin had invited us to the wake afterwards at a nearby hotel, but we declined. We weren't family and it didn't seem right to intrude.

"Have you considered why he's so curmudgeonly?"

Aunt Madge asked as she cut a fruit cake into slices then poured piping hot tea from the pot.

I shook my head. "Laurie said Mr Norton was a pacifist. That doesn't ring true with his obnoxiousness, though."

"It's not only the men who fought in those two wars who suffer from delayed shock and stress, you know. The medics, the doctors, nurses, ambulance drivers, the firefighters. The ordinary sea merchantmen, anyone who with extreme bravery took a little boat over to Dunkirk. The secret service – on the front line and behind the scenes. So many of us have so many memories that we would rather forget, but cannot."

"Even you?"

She nodded solemnly. "Even me. I did my job for the war, as did Toby. But not all of it was pleasant. Our work saved a lot of lives, yes, but equally it sent many men and women to their deaths. And not easy deaths, at that. There's many a veteran who cannot shake off an unwanted memory. Many a civilian who, even now, flinches at an unexpected sound."

She thought for a while, then said, "I came across this poem not long ago:

> "See that grumpy old man over there?
> I used to laugh and snigger when the
>   toaster popped when he was unaware.
> He used to jump out of his skin and
>   shiver.
> I never understood when I got told to
>   stop, but it was funny to me.
> One day when I was eighteen, I spoke to
>   that grumpy old man.
> I was proud to tell him I had signed up
>   for the army.
> He sat me down and said to me,

'My boy I have never spoken of the past,
and you never did understand why the
toaster made me jump.
For I was a soldier and one day you will
fully understand.'
He told me about his life.
He said, 'I boarded that ship and
thought,
will I ever see my loved one and my
English homeland again?'
I went through pain every day, fighting
for my life, regiment, and country.
We were frightened men in the trenches,
cold, wet, hungry with dying men
around us.
But I will not speak of it today.'
I knew he was not telling me everything,
he continued to say:
'One day the guns fell silent on that
battlefield,
a silence not known but only dreamt of.
For the war was over, I had survived,
I was going home with my head held
high,
for I am the one who served my country
for you to live and thrive today.'
He never spoke of any of it again.
He passed away a few years later, and
only now do I realise
what that grumpy old man meant.
For I am now a veteran, watching my son
at sports day,
And they laughed at me when I jumped
and hid under my chair
when the starting gun fired.
Only now do I realise that in a soldier's

mind a bang could be a grenade or
sniper.
If only I knew back then why that
grumpy old man jumped and
shivered
And why sullen temper was his
protective shield.
For today, tomorrow and all days to
come, do not let shadows and
memories
of our soldiers die, for they are our
heroes,
honour, respect and remember them.
And don't condemn or laugh.
You do not know their past."

My guilt increased tenfold. Mr Norton always complained about the noise from the next door TV. Especially the *bang, bang, bang* of the guns in those westerns. No wonder he hated them!

"That's a lovely poem," I said, to hide my shame, and wiping a tear from the corner of my eye, asked, "Who wrote it?"

Aunt Madge topped up her cup of tea and helped herself to another slice of cake.

"I've no idea, it's 'anon'. It was written as a eulogy for a dear friend who could not stop being afraid of loud noises after being shelled in the trenches."

I didn't answer. Words did not seem appropriate, but I did wonder about Mr Norton. Perhaps I had made a mistake about him? Grumpy, short tempered, no patience and no tolerance? Hardly surprising when you knew a background reason.

I made a couple of decisions that afternoon. Sort of late New Year Resolutions.

One. I'd try harder to be understanding about things.

Two. When I had it finished to my satisfaction, I would ask Mr Norton if he would take a look at my science fiction manuscript. For an honest opinion.

Three. If he rubbished it and tore it apart, I would be brave and take it on the chin.

Four. If he had a few good words to say, then I'd know he wasn't just being nice.

26

MY FAULT?

Poor Miss Catesby's funeral the next day was very different.

The vicar, me, Aunt Madge, Uncle Toby and Laurie, the next door neighbour and her husband, and the heir and his wife, the son of Miss Catesby's fiancé's brother. A complicated relationship, a fact which he, Julian Barrowstone, acknowledged after the funeral was over. A quiet, simple burial in a shady corner of Chingford Cemetery.

I couldn't help dwelling on the fact that she'd died because of me, although, when I voiced my guilt that morning, Aunt Madge had told me off, and said that Joe Briggs was to blame, not me.

"But I told him I'd left my ring at her house. I told him she was an elderly lady on her own– I even told him where she lived, so it *is* all my fault."

She had put her hands on my arms and given me a gentle shake. "No it is not. He was stalking you, probably with the intention of robbing you at some point. Or he might have just been deluded that you liked him. He was lucky, you inadvertently told him some useful information and he twisted your words into his own criminal intentions. You are not responsible for his actions. Only he is."

She was right, but I found it hard to believe her.

"He made a habit of following vulnerable women, Jan. He'd done it once or twice and found it was easy. In time, if he hadn't been caught, who knows how he might have expanded his operation? Young women, not the elderly, chatting them up, apparently being nice until he backed them into a corner. He's the sort of slimeball who can be oh-so charming until he doesn't get his own way, or what he wants. Then his true character comes out."

There was no wake. Mr Barrowstone had not known who might attend, so had made no plans.

"Is there anywhere we could go for a cup of tea and a sandwich?" he offered.

Laurie and Uncle Toby had to get back to work, and Aunt Madge, being Aunt Madge, refused to consider anywhere except home, so invited Mr and Mrs Barrowstone and the neighbours back to our house. How she managed to rustle up a heaped pile of sandwiches *and* a chocolate cake without batting an eyelid I've never managed to figure out. Perhaps it was all a part of debutante training? Or, she had been a Girl Guide, so was always 'Be Prepared'. Or was that the Scouts motto?

The neighbours did not stay long, I think they felt a bit awkward, but Mr Barrowstone – Julian as we were soon calling him – and his wife, Sarah, stayed a good while, chatting and finding out as much as they could from the little I was able to tell them. Julian had, genuinely, no idea of his possible aunt-by-marriage's existence. Such a shame because she would have so enjoyed his company.

Assuming the inheritance probate went through without difficulty, they intended to sell the house, donate some of the money to charity and, intrigued by my tale of Miss Catesby's Albert, they jumped at Aunt Madge's suggestion of SSAFA, the Soldiers, Sailors, Airmen and Families Association as a suitable recipient. SSAFA was the oldest of the UK's national tri-service Armed Forces charity. Miss Catesby would have been so pleased at that decision. They also insisted that I keep Poppy. They had two dogs, and didn't think a cat would be welcome. I was relieved at that, Poppy was a dear little cat, and had settled in with us so well.

As they were leaving, Julian kissed my cheek and thanked me again, then made an offer which brought tears to my eyes.

"Look," he said, "I'm sure that Aunt Mary," (as he was now, fondly, calling Miss Catesby), "would have wanted you to have something of hers. I've to go through all the legal paraphernalia and such, but assuming all goes well, is there anything you would like from the house as a memento?"

I was thrilled, and choked at the same time. Knew exactly what to ask for.

"Can I have the photograph of Miss Catesby's Albert please? She treasured that picture, and I'd treasure it just as much."

What I didn't say, was that I wanted a reminder to always treasure what *I* had. My Laurie, in case I ever lost him.

27

INTERLUDE - DS LAURIE WALKER

The Isle of Wight didn't seem particularly white to me. Mind, because of the rain, I couldn't see much of it across the Solent, save for a vague blurred outline. I think the entire country was sick of the alternating downpours with constant drizzle. There had been some flooding in a few places in England, poor souls, there's nothing worse than being flooded out. Well, except being burned to the ground I suppose.

I wasn't in a congenial mood as I walked into the Hampshire Station and asked for DCI Murray, the man I was to liaise with. I was tired, it had been a long, frustrating drive with far too many hold-ups and I was a good hour behind the time of my expected arrival. The Isle of Wight, though an autonomous county, had been amalgamated with Hampshire Constabulary as a war time measure in 1943, but with so many of these things, despite the usual platitudes and assurances that the measure would be reversed come peacetime, it never was. By 1948 the I.O.W. Constabulary had been totally absorbed into Hampshire.

DCI Murray had given up waiting for me, so I met DS Wally Stanbrook instead, which was, perhaps, a blessing as Murray, I discovered, had the reputation of being unhelpful if he thought unwelcome boots were tramping on his patch. Which was rather irritating as I had no intention of stamping anywhere.

All I wanted was to find Kevin Young and ask him a few questions about the afternoon of the murder of Gerald Duffield.

"Is he a suspect?" Stanbrook asked me over a pleasant pint and even pleasanter game pie with lashings of gravy, partaken of at a decent seafront pub. It was evening, I'd put my travel bag in my room at the hotel I'd booked into, and joined Stanbrook for dinner. We'd be catching the ferry across to the Island first thing in the morning.

"Suspect? Not really, no more than the others on our list. George Duffield the brother, Paul Norton the neighbour, possibly the cousin – but there'd be no financial gain there, it's George who owns the house, not Gerald, so if that was the motivation, they killed the wrong man."

"You say the brothers didn't get on?"

I wiped my mouth with the paper napkin, the gravy really was delicious. "Hated each other. The house ownership was possibly another bone of contention between the two of them. George is, was, the eldest twin. I rather think that Gerald had an 'heir and spare' sort of complex, plus it was George who had most of the attention because of his war heroics." I filled Wally in about that.

"Well we've discreetly located Young, as your DCI requested. He's at a hostel a few miles from Ryde. Been around several places, fishing he says, must be barmy in this weather. When you interview him, ask him what he's caught. Might catch him out if he names the wrong fish."

I jotted the right types that he gave me down in my

notebook and spent the rest of the evening enjoying the beer, the company and a couple of good games of darts. I let Stanbrook win the first game, then discovered that he was a decent player – and a decent copper – so I played as well as I could. Won three, lost two.

Believe it or not, the morning was bright and clear with only a few wispy clouds hovering over the Island. Stanbrook met me as arranged, in his car, and we took the ferry across the short stretch of water. A tad cold and blustery, but the fresh air certainly blew the cobwebs and a slight hangover away. I'd been to the Isle of Wight as a child, happy memories of splashing in the sea, building sandcastles and collecting layers of different coloured sand from the cliffs, scraping the sand with a blunt knife into a three-inch glass vial shaped like a lighthouse, which Mum bought me from the tourist shop. I still had it, stoppered once filled, in my bedroom back home in Devon. I don't know if they still allowed people to do this or not, never had the chance to find out, but in hindsight, as far as erosion was concerned, I don't suppose letting hundreds, thousands maybe, of tourists loose to scrape away at the cliffs, no matter how pretty the result, was a good idea.

I found Kevin Young at his breakfast, a late breakfast, 'brunch' I think it's called, for it was not far off 11 a.m. He'd had more of a night drinking and enjoying himself than I had. Maybe that was the lure of fishing, not the fish? He scowled when he saw and recognised me, but I had the impression that he scowled at everyone.

"What are you doing here? What do you want?" he growled as I sat down opposite him. "My bloody wife sent you, has she? Well, you can go back and tell her I've left her. Had enough of her, I have. I'm stayin' right 'ere."

"Just a few questions; seeing if you could help us with our enquiries about the murder of Gerald Duffield."

"Who? Never heard of 'im. You accusing me?" He snarled.

"No, not at all, it's just that you were in the area at the time and we wondered if you could recall seeing anyone hanging around." I explained who I was talking about. "Gerald Duffield. Leawood Avenue. The Tuesday you drove the library van."

"Nothin' t'do with me, mate."

"Maybe you know his brother, George?" This was like pulling teeth.

Young scraped a last piece of fried bread round his egg and baked-bean leftovers plate, then admitted, "I do know that bloke Norton. He shouts a lot, comes out to moan about the van parked outside his 'ouse."

"George and Gerald Duffield are twins. They live next door to Norton. They share the same house. Miss Christopher delivers books to all three of them."

"None the wiser, mate."

"George is always talking about westerns and trains. His brother lives upstairs."

Young scratched at his stubbled chin, shook his head. "Nope. I'm blank. Which one was done in then? The train guy or the other one?"

"The other one. Could you tell me what you did that day, so we can officially eliminate you from our enquiries? I've come a long way, Mr Young."

He sniffed, wiped a splodge of egg from his chin. Seemed more co-operative now. "I met you at the library's back door. Took the young lady out on her round – and she took her time with some of the old goats, I can tell you. Talks too much, she does. We went for a cuppa at that church place, I realised I'd not locked the van door and ran back to see to it. Can't trust things nowadays. Not enough decent coppers on the beat to keep an eye on things, is there? I locked the van, hopped into the bushes beside that Baptist Church for a Jimmy Riddle, and had to wait for some old girl to mess about with locking the church door. Now, she went off in the direction of that house. Maybe she saw someone?"

I shook my head. "We've already spoken to her, she didn't see you, or anyone or anything."

Young sat back in his chair, shrugged then folded his arms over his belly. "Well there you are then, like I said, I made sure I were hidden in them bushes, and no one else was around. I can't help you. Sorry. You sure my damn wife ain't sent you? I'm not going back to 'er. Got m'self a job down here. Driving job."

So that was that. I had no inclination to believe him about the job, but his domestic arrangements were none of my business. I politely thanked him, said I hoped he'd enjoy the rest of his fishing, crossed back to the mainland with Wally, collected my car and drove all the way back to North London.

I didn't like Kevin Young, but, as I'd said to Jan, not liking someone did not make them a murderer.

28

BACK TO WORK

I had two weeks off work from the library, during which time, apart from the two funerals, I managed to write about three chapters of my novel and played with Poppy, who was such a sweetie, a contrast to Bruiser Basil. Although, having said that, he was a Contrary Mary. Normally Basil would have absolutely *nothing* to do with any other puss; he frequently came home with bitten ears and lumps of fur missing from where he'd been in a punch-up. With Poppy, he adopted her as his ward, his responsibility. Apart from occasions when she was annoying him because she wanted to play and he didn't. Then, he was quite happy to disown her.

I was making lunchtime sandwiches in the kitchen (I was getting quite proficient at doing things one-handed, and using my plaster cast arm as an anchor). Basil was curled asleep beside the Aga, which this time of year was kept on at a low heat to keep the kitchen cosy – to help out the cranky central heating that (supposedly) warmed the rest of the house. He was curled the way cats do, with his front paws neatly tucked in, head down, asleep. Poppy had found a ping-pong ball and was ping-ponging it round the kitchen, batting it off appliances and cupboards, making quite a clatter as she did so. I noticed the tip of Basil's tail start to twitch. Then the inevitable happened. Poppy pinged it right into the fold of his paws.

Basil didn't move. Slowly, slowly, he opened one eye, then the other. He looked at Poppy. Looked at the ball. Looked at the refrigerator and the small gap beneath it. Looked again at the ball. Casually, leisurely, he extended one paw and then quickly and neatly bopped the ping-pong ball across the floor and straight into the gap beneath the fridge. He then re-curled his paw, closed his eyes and went back to sleep. If he were one of the England football team, he'd have been feted for such magnificent goal scoring.

Poor Poppy was devastated. Me? I couldn't help but laugh. I relented, though, picked her up and found her another ball to play with in the sitting room. (Which she promptly lost beneath the sofa.)

I was bored. I had plenty to do; books to read, my own to write. TV, radio. A jigsaw to finish. I liked jigsaws as long as they were not too hard or complicated. This one was of Queen Elizabeth II riding her favourite black mare, Burmese, side-saddle at the Trooping of the Colour ceremony. There were a lot of red and black pieces of Busby-wearing red-coated soldiers to slot together.

I'd seen Burmese when the Royal Canadian Mounted Police who had bred her presented her to the Queen as a gift. In April 1969 the Mounties had organised a wonderful demonstration musical ride at Windsor Horse Show, with Burmese as one of the horses involved in the display. The Queen had asked if the rider would carry her Royal Standard instead of their usual red and white pennon, so that she – and we, the audience – could follow the correct horse as all the

Mounties' horses looked the same, beautiful black animals. The following year Aunt Madge and I were in the crowd at Horse Guards, watching the actual Trooping of the Colour parade, and saw Her Majesty riding Burmese side-saddle. Both, unforgettable occasions.

Aunt Madge rarely mentioned that she had been a debutante presented to the Royal Family, including the then Princess Elizabeth, at Queen Charlotte's Ball in 1942. The ball was named after King George III's beloved wife, Charlotte of Mecklenburg-Strelitz, with that first ball held in honour of her birthday, where she stood beside a giant birthday cake and the debutantes all curtseyed to her. Ostensibly, the ball was designed to raise funds for charity, one of which was the founding of the Queen Charlotte's and Chelsea Hospital for Women. Aunt Madge still had the exquisite tulle and silk Dior dress that she'd worn (and could still fit into) at the 1942 ball she'd attended, *and* she could curtsy correctly. It's quite a knack to put one leg behind the other, sink slowly and then rise again without wobbling. I might add that Aunt Madge had taught me, and I could do a perfect curtsy. Alas I didn't have any suitable events to attend where I could use it. It was highly unlikely that I would ever meet the Queen. And by the way, Aunt Madge could also ride aside – side-saddle. (Not boasting – OK, I am – I can ride side-saddle too.)

Laurie had spent two days away looking for our library van driver in order to interview him – in the vain hope that he might have seen something or someone. When Laurie got home from the Isle of Wight, he was in a melancholy mood because the trip had been a waste of time. It didn't look like we were ever going to find the person who killed Gerald Duffield, and I was still anxious that my uncle, and

Laurie, suspected George. I must admit, I was beginning to wonder if they were right.

After the two weeks I went back to work. Plaster cast (adorned with various signatures and doodles) an' all. Some things on that first day, Monday, were a bit awkward to do one-handed, but I managed serving at the counter and shelving books, which I did by wheeling the trolley one-handed and making good use of my hip. Everything took me longer to do, and I had to explain to almost everyone who came in what had happened. One lovely gentleman even came back with a bunch of flowers and a get well soon card.

Uncle Toby, Laurie or Aunt Madge were to pick me up every evening as I didn't feel confident about using the bus, even though I knew *He* would not be there, and anyway, I was exhausted. Once back home that first day, I had dinner and went straight to bed. Tuesday, my second day, was to be my B.D.S. round again.

I selected the books I needed by making use of the trolley as I couldn't carry armfuls, and our Librarian, Pamela, had arranged for Harry to help me with the actual round. He was such a dear, and made no fuss or bluster about carrying the books into the houses for me. Actually, I think he enjoyed it, for he loved to talk.

I filled him in with everything that had happened, and I was more than a little trepidatious about going in to see George Duffield when we got there.

I need not have worried. He was fine. It was almost as if nothing had happened, he'd even let the upstairs flat to the young cousin, or whatever relation he was, who had started work at the Town Hall, and who kept an eye on him, did the shopping, loved watching westerns and was organising a suitable hearing aid for George to use. So everything had worked out well for the both of them.

George tutted sympathetically over my cast and added his name to my collection – signing as 'Yee Ha George'. Of his brother, the murder, the funeral, of anything else, not a word. Which made me wonder even harder. There was no remorse, no grief, nothing beyond the strong feeling that George was pleased to be rid of his brother at last.

My previous call to Mr Paul Norton had been of a different nature. I'd decided not to say anything, yet, about my scribblings, which was just as well as he complained about being interviewed by the police, complained about their to-ing and fro-ing, their impertinence and 'poking about in people's private lives,' as he put it.

Harry, bless him, countered this tirade with a stern word. "Forgive me for saying, sir, but a man was brutally murdered, surely you would welcome the diligence of the police to ensure your safety? Given that the culprit is not yet discovered, there is every chance he might come back for whatever it was he wanted in the first place. For all we know, he made a mistake. Got the wrong house, killed the wrong man."

That shut Mr Norton up. He turned quite pale.

"And surely," I had added, wearing my sweetest smile, "you want to ensure that your name is entirely cleared from any potential suspect list?"

"My dear girl," he'd blustered back, now turning quite red, "I assure you that I am no murderer!"

Still smiling, I retaliated with, "My uncle, DCI Christopher, says that all criminals say 'it weren't me guv' just like they do on the telly." Needless to say, Uncle Toby had said no such thing.

Was Mr Norton a suspect? Laurie had never said anything beyond general talk, but then, he hadn't discussed the case with me lately as there was nothing to discuss. Except, I didn't think he would have been happy about me delivering books to a suspected murderer, even with Harry accompanying me as a makeshift bodyguard. But then, Laurie *had* been overprotective lately. I found it stifling, to be honest. I wasn't a child any more. And while I did appreciate his frequent asking, "Are you all right?" it was becoming somewhat tedious.

Harry and I were welcomed at the Church Hall, and offered free tea and cake, in return for first hand insider knowledge of what had happened and how far forward the police were in their investigations. I could only be truthful and say, "Not far at all," but I did reassure the volunteer tea ladies that they were quite safe. The man responsible for the burglaries, and death of poor Miss Catesby who had lived only a few minutes' walk away at the other end of the alley running beside the church, was well and truly behind bars and would stay there for some while. Or at least, so I hoped.

Friday Hill Library was to be our last call. I'd be returning to the library much earlier than usual, what with two people fewer to call on, their replacements not yet made. Harry and I had eked out our tea break for as long as we could, and I'd counted on delaying for another ten or fifteen minutes at Friday Hill Library. Mrs Colchester didn't let us down.

"Is there any chance," she said, beaming at me and Harry – well Harry – as we walked in, "that you could fiddle with the bolt on the lavatory door? It's come loose and, well, I'm wary of making use of it while we're open and I cannot lock it. I don't want an unexpected embarrassing 'half mast' situation. And sitting and singing is not entirely the answer. One lady asked if I was having a heart attack." She laughed, I wasn't sure if she was joking or not.

Harry went to inspect the lock, then went out to the

van. He came back, looking quite cross, which was unusual for Harry.

"Some blighter's been down my screwdrivers," he grumbled, opening the red plastic case and showing the contents with one empty space. One of the screwdrivers clearly missing.

I stood there, dumbstruck. There was only one explanation.

29

FISH, CHIPS AND MURDER

Kevin Young was arrested a day later by the Isle of Wight Police Force, and brought to Chingford in handcuffs. From what Laurie told me, the fishing holiday had not gone well, there was no expected job and he'd told no one of his intention to stay on the Isle of Wight. Not the council, nor his wife. The council, as it turned out, had already given him notice for frequently not turning up to work. His wife was furious because he'd left her with no money – Laurie told me that when she visited him at Chingford Police Station she slapped him so hard it resulted in a black eye, and her only interest in seeing the man was to demand a divorce.

Most of what had really happened on that fateful B.D.S. round day Laurie and my uncle had managed to piece together bit by bit. They revealed all at the weekend, the Saturday evening, once they had enough irrefutable evidence to charge Kevin Young with the murder of Gerald Duffield. I again felt partly to blame, for I'd put my foot well and truly 'in it'.

Laurie fetched in fish and chips and we sat round

the dining room table, the fire blazing with sweet-scented apple tree logs, candles on the mantlepiece and table lit. (Aunt Madge had her standards, even for lowly Chippy Tea.). Basil and Poppy curled together on the hearthrug, one eye open for any stray flakes of cod.

"Kevin Young," Uncle Toby explained, "was eight years old when his mother died. His father was a POW, taken prisoner at Dunkirk, he died in one of the stalags in 1944. Kevin and his older sister were evacuated to Cornwall, to his grandparents – his father's people – who lived in Truro. The couple were staunch churchgoers, with the grandfather a stickler for discipline. The slightest misdemeanour would result in the belt or a birching. It was a miserable time, only lightened on the few occasions when the mother came to visit. She worked in one of the big London stores, hadn't wanted children, had no intention of giving up her job or lifestyle. From what I gather, she was pleased to be rid of the kids."

Laurie groaned as he smacked the bottom of the glass bottle of Heinz Ketchup and too much tomato sauce shot out all over his chips. He took up the tale. "The mother was expected but she never turned up. Later, the police arrived to say that she was dead, killed in an unavoidable train accident."

My mouth dropped open. "Not George Duffield's train!"

"Mmm hmm," Uncle Toby said, reaching for the sauce but not smacking the bottle quite so hard. "George Duffield's train. The children had to remain with the grandparents and had a miserable life. The sister had to get married at sixteen to a salesman, and went off up North with him. Young joined up as soon as he was old enough to do his National Service, then bummed around doing various jobs. Married – also by

necessity – and ended up as a council driver. He knew the details of how his mother had died, that she'd fatally split her skull open when a train, being attacked by a German plane, had high-tailed it into a convenient tunnel and slammed on the emergency brakes. The driver, George, was a hero. Kevin hated him, blamed him for the misery of his endured childhood with grandparents who had not an ounce of love or compassion in them. Knew the name, but had no idea where the man was, or even whether he was still alive."

Laurie took over the story. "He nursed a grudge against that train driver for all these years. Then one day, in total innocence..."

I steadied myself with a gulp of the white wine and continued for Laurie. "Then one day, totally out of the blue, a library assistant told him about an old man who loved reading westerns and who used to work for Great Western Railway and who repeatedly told the story of his one claim to fame."

"That's right, I'm afraid. But don't you dare go blaming yourself, Cupcake." Uncle Toby topped up my wine glass. "He says that his intention was to have it out with the old boy, make it clear that he should know what he'd done."

"But," I said butting in, "not knowing there were two twin brothers he killed the wrong man by mistake. Killed Gerald, not George."

"On the pretence of not locking the van, he went to the house, which he knew from watching you go in; knocked at the door. An elderly man answered. Young said something like, 'You the train driver?' and the chap started yelling. Young confessed that he was walking away, but the man followed, cursing and swearing about trains and medals. He felt in his pocket, found the screwdriver he'd been using to unstick the van's ashtray and next thing, it was in the old man. Unfortunately, a man nursing such latent anger should never have been in the forces, conscripted or not."

Laurie stayed for the evening. He was still bruised from Joe's assault, but we cuddled up together in the small back room, playing records. I'd retrieved my engagement ring from Aunt Madge (she'd long ago removed it from her handbag and put it safe, in the house safe), but my fingers were still puffy so I'd threaded it on a silver chain and wore it round my neck.

"Are you sure about marrying me?" he suddenly said as he turned an LP over to play the flip side.

It took me rather by surprise. "What makes you ask?" I answered, stalling for time and something sensible to say.

He shrugged. "You've been distant, not as bubbly as usual and I..." he faltered, then went on boldly, "and I wouldn't want you to make a mistake."

He looked so crestfallen, so desperately dejected.

I got up from the sofa and waved my plaster cast in the air. "I *have* been slightly distracted," I pointed out, "but, well, truthfully? I've not been sure about marrying a policeman. I know what it's like when night after night someone has to work late on a case. I know, first hand, the danger, the worry, and that one day, one day you might not come home. So I've been doubting. Do I really, really, want that?"

"Jan..."

"I haven't finished. Maybe, yes, us getting married might turn out to be a mistake, but we don't know what will happen in the future, and whatever *does* happen, I don't want to discover that the biggest mistake I ever made was losing you, the man I love. Even if he is a bossy policeman with a bald patch at the back of his head where he had several stitches because some demented nutter hit him."

POSTSCRIPT

Writing these memoir recollections these many years later after I'd come across my old diaries in the attic during the long days of Covid lockdown in 2020, has resurrected the pleasure of those past years when I was young, naïve and in love.

Murder is not a pleasant subject to write about is it? But you can't be involved with policemen and ignore the nasty side of life. The one, sadly, goes with the other. What can't be ignored is truth, loyalty and love. And I think I have just the right amount of that to have survived all these years relatively unscathed.

I miss my days of working in the library. I miss my old ladies and gentlemen, although I guess I am now as old as they were, but I have the fortune of not being housebound. I did, a few years ago, make a list of books I would want to read if ever I were in need of a Book Delivery Service. I threw the list away a couple of Christmases ago when my daughter bought me a Kindle. They are wonderful for instantly obtaining books – but they don't do the washing up like I used to do for dear old Miss Catesby.

And Laurie never did, quite, lose that small bald patch on the back of his head.

Until next time,

Jan

AUTHOR'S NOTE AND ACKNOWLEDGEMENTS

This is a work of fiction, all the characters are entirely made up, but for those interested in detail: South Chingford Branch Library was a real library. The building (at the time of writing this – 2022/3) is still there in Hall Lane, but it is no longer a library. I worked there from 1969 when I left Wellington Avenue Secondary School for Girls at the age of sixteen, until 1982. I have many memories – some good, some not so good; such is life when working for the public.

As much as I have been able, I have checked and researched the various details mentioned about the early 1970s to ensure they are accurate. I cannot guarantee I have everything right, however. Memory is not always reliable, and as much as I hate to accept it, the 1970s were a long time ago.

My thanks to two ladies who went to the same school as me, Wellington Avenue: Janet for her recollection of the policeman and the hats – the incident had nothing to do with me, but was such a good anecdote I had to use it. And to Sheila for her recollection of her mum, Flo, working in the canteen at Chingford police station. I'm not sure if sausage sandwiches were on the menu, nor whether there were reproduction paintings on the wall, but it *was* a small canteen, and the floor lino was brown. My thanks to the two of you for letting me use your memories.

The 69 bus ran via Walthamstow Central underground and overhead railway station to the railway and bus termini in Station Road, North Chingford, and was a regular bus that I used. I heartily thank a few people from our school social media group who confirmed my memory of the bus – and the fare of 5p. So thank you Alan, Christine, Mark, Paul and Beverley.

I vaguely remember a rather chilly Old Church hall atop Chingford Mount (not the lovely one that is there now), but as far as I know the church ladies did not do afternoon teas with cake, so I made this up. Friday Hill Library was much appreciated by the residents of Friday Hill, but it was eventually closed to save money. Mrs Colchester is based on the librarian who worked there. She was, as I have depicted, a lovely lady. The Sirloin Pub was always known as this, but I have been informed that it now has a different name. What a shame; thus, a charming and cheerful local legend is erased.

I must mention money. A £5 note went a long way back in 1972, today the equivalent would be a little over £70. My first pay packet in 1969 was just over £100. I thought I was rich.

A quick thank you to Cathy Helms for her patience and expertise for designing the cover and for formatting the text. To the wonderful ladies who read through early versions and especially thank you to Annie Whitehead. Errors are all my own doing.

I must mention the photograph on the cover. It's my Dad. A personal little tribute to a fine man.

My daughter Kathy wrote the poem about the old soldier. I've blatantly stolen it.

Finally, I began writing the Jan Christopher Mystery series during the 2020/21 lockdowns of the Covid-19 pandemic as I wanted to write something different from my usual novels. The challenge proved most enjoyable then, and remains so now.

There will be more Jan Christopher Mysteries to solve...

Helen Hollick
2023

SOUTH CHINGFORD LIBRARY

South Chingford Library, Hall Lane
As it is today – offices.
Photo: with thanks to author ©Alison Morton

ABOUT THE AUTHOR

Helen Hollick and her family moved from north-east London in January 2013 after finding an eighteenth-century North Devon farmhouse through being a 'victim' on BBC TV's popular *Escape To The Country* show. The thirteen-acre property was the first one she was shown – and it was love at first sight. She enjoys her new rural life, and has a variety of animals on the farm, including Exmoor ponies and her daughter's string of show jumpers, pigs, hens, ducks and geese (and the cats and dogs).

First accepted for publication by William Heinemann in 1993 – a week after her fortieth birthday – Helen then became a USA Today Bestseller with her historical novel, *The Forever Queen* (titled *A Hollow Crown* in the UK) with the sequel, *Harold the King* (US: *I Am The Chosen King*) being novels that explore the events that led to the Battle of Hastings in 1066. Her *Pendragon's Banner Trilogy* is a fifth-century version of the Arthurian legend, and she also writes a pirate-based nautical adventure/fantasy series, *The Sea Witch Voyages*. Despite being impaired by the visual disorder of glaucoma, she is also branching out into the quick read novella, 'Cosy Mystery' genre with the *Jan Christopher Mysteries,* set in the 1970s, with the first in the series, *A Mirror Murder* incorporating her, often hilarious, memories of working for thirteen years as a library assistant.

Her non-fiction books are *Pirates: Truth and Tales* and *Life of A Smuggler*. She also runs her own blog, a News and Events blog for her village – and occasionally gets time to write...

Website: www.helenhollick.net
Amazon Author Page (Universal Link):
http://viewauthor.at/HelenHollick
Newsletter Subscription:
http://tinyletter.com/HelenHollick
Blog: www.ofhistoryandkings.blogspot.com
Mastodon: https://mastodonapp.uk/@HelenHollick
Facebook: www.facebook.com/HelenHollickAuthor
Twitter: @HelenHollick

ALSO BY HELEN HOLLICK

THE PENDRAGON'S BANNER TRILOGY

The Kingmaking: Book One

Pendragon's Banner: Book Two

Shadow of the King: Book Three

THE SAXON 1066 SERIES

A Hollow Crown (UK edition title)

The Forever Queen (US edition title. USA Today bestseller)

Harold the King (UK edition title)

I Am The Chosen King (US edition title)

1066 Turned Upside Down

(alternative short stories by various authors)

THE SEA WITCH VOYAGES OF

CAPTAIN JESAMIAH ACORNE

Sea Witch: The first voyage

Pirate Code: The second voyage

Bring It Close: The third voyage

Ripples In The Sand: The fourth voyage

On The Account: The fifth voyage

Gallows Wake: The sixth voyage

When The Mermaid Sings

A short read prequel to the Sea Witch Voyages

Coffee Pot Book Club Book of the Year 2022

BRONZE AWARD WINNER

To follow

Jamaica Gold: The seventh voyage

BETRAYAL

Short stories by various authors

(including a Jesamiah Acorne adventure)

NON-FICTION

Pirates: Truth and Tales

Life Of A Smuggler: In Fact And Fiction

BEFORE YOU GO

How To Say 'Thank you' to your favourite authors (Feedback is so important, and we do appreciate your comments.)

Leave a review on Amazon
http://viewauthor.at/HelenHollick

'Like' and 'follow' where you can

Subscribe to a newsletter

Buy a copy of your favourite book as a present

Spread the word!

Printed in Great Britain
by Amazon

23298292R00101